Before its all said and done. This story will make you feel like you've been hit over the head with a iron skillet! But take heart its just the process. Still that's how this case has made me feel trying to piece it all together! And as they say in all the best generic movies ever made...and so it begins.

It was a cold dark winter night. Kinda like this one when I got the call. Outside it was raining cats and dogs on the city of Hopeful North Carolina! Seems ol' Mustard head (real name) Garner Alfred Musterini. Mustard for short, don't ask. And my boss, down at the prescient. Was pulling double duty tonight. His wife Gloria just so happened to be going into labor in all this bad weather! Which makes perfectly good sense since the fat faced bald headed guy was a blow hard! His jet powered Chevy was rampted up on maximum speed, burning all cylinders! And was breaking new records around the eleven o'clock hour in the middle of the night. With sweat pouring down into his already drenched clothing from the rain. And his wife stretched out on the back seat calling on Jesus! No one could make the argument that he wasn't cutting those curves like a pro! Just exactly around the same time he zoomed in front her door. It always irked me that he could never remember "her" name for shit! But that was my hang up not his, when it came to stuff like this! I had to suddenly stop typing right here, since my old injury from when I was a boy started kicking up again. My hands stiffened bone straight with crippling arthritis before turning my knuckles into mutilated dog paws! The cramps was so bad I threw down as much whiskey with my other hand a man could handle. Yeah I was a mess! I had a headache coming on to boot that this liquor bottle couldn't fix! Again my hang ups my worry. I peered down into the streets watching the moon glistening into a muddy puddle on its way to becoming a pothole. I felt compelled to blame myself for getting involved time and time again in lost causes! Because had I'd known how deep I would have buried myself in this pile of shit? I would have walked away!

At The Sienna Club (Jan. 3 2016)

Part 1

Sunday morning although as gray as the day is long. Didn't stop the good citizens of Hopeful from cramming themselves into their favorite place of worship. Strong Hope Missionary Baptist Church, had over a thousand members and counting. Pastor Lonnie Bradford briskly read from the passages of his favorite Scriptures today. The one he enjoyed the most. The book of Psalms. He didn't preach his usual fanfare of fire and brimstone damnation either. Neither did he delve head long into the soul stirring passages of Revelations. Nor did he hoop and holler his throat sore from the rousing book of Eli. No, not today. Instead today his teachings was founded in a more recognizable sort for most people. A text more subtle and serene. As he leaned over the pulpit teaching more then preaching the beautiful scriptures of King Solomon. Mira Sylvester walked through the double doors. She was wearing a over the knee crisp and clean dark blue form fitting skirt. It complimented very well the simply stated short sleeve starch white blouse. The thing was so clean like they say it must be Tide! The clothes could perhaps be thought under stated but never the woman. It matched the elegant beauty's body to perfection. And the pink cameo she paired with it. The brooch clasped neatly in place at the neck kept probing eyes out her ample bosom. The patent leather purse she clutched in her hand, was the same as the black patent leather heels hardly she wore that hardly made a sound. Mira's long black shiny curly hair had that blunt cut to it, it hung to the middle of her back. And easily accentuated her beautiful oval face. She was a modern day fashion plate. Today her hair swung freely underneath a small powdered light blue feather hat with a tiny dark blue veil attached to it. Her gloves impeccable. They was dark blue velvet as if there to make a statement. Mira Sylvester was a womanly jewel and I was in love with her.

Of course everybody turned around, the moment the temptress walked through the door. The sour air coming off some of those women was putrid to say the least. Enough to leave a bad taste in the mouth! And you could have cut the tension in the air as they say, with a Swiss army blade when she passed each one. "What is she even doing here?" One of the choir members scoffs. "I don't know!" the other grumbled. Maybe she's confused the church with the Sienna Club again." They enjoyed their joke at Mira's expense. Both giggled noisily until a stern looking Deaconess wop them upside the head with her fan! Seeing that ..the rest of the choir members thought it best to remain mum. Pastor Lonnie Bradford had cleared his throat when he spotted Mira come in. He was the town's under cover freak! So I was told. And under the influence of one of those lustful spirits he raved about! I heard a rumor that the good looking pastor had also been stalking some of those young christian ladies in a not so very christian way. Still again, not my circus not my monkeys. Although it was evident that he did have a pretty healthy appetite for the ladies. And Mira was definitely a pretty woman. Folks in the vicinity told me he was a skirt chaser and I chose to believe them! The thirty two year old man was my age. He was called cute cut and fine by some of those questionable young ladies! You'd swear he had groupies from the way they followed him around after church! And like it or not his youthful face did bring in a significant amount of young folks to the Church when there parents obviously could not! And besides that there was no denying he was the Church's cash cow! The church payroll was testament to that! The profits made the church wealthier and wealthier, with him then without him! And the church knew that! So in there laid as they say, their bone of constriction.

"He gotta go!" Was the final agreement, among the so called saved members of Hopeful Baptist Church. Shit the man was the main reason they became a mega-Church in the first place, wasn't he? So I couldn't wrap my brain cells around anybody cutting off their own nose to spite their face! Come hell or high water! The dude days was certainly numbered! The older members of the church quietly sat their plan in motion. Or should I say their righteous execution of a young pastor's demise! The man wasn't married and had no intentions of doing so. Just to satisfy a old outdated seniors planned agenda! He just wanted to keep right on with his interaction and indiscretions. And wining and dining their lovely daughters without consequence! Oh he knew he was sinning! And was a man of the cloth. But as long as those young ladies entertained his foolish addition, how could he stop! So secretly the elder members met with other Pastors from various churches. They wanted a more settled Pastor for their church and one more mature. Over sixty five and married would do just fine! Mira rolled her eyes at him when she became aware of him ogling her legs! But it would be those dark lines running up the back of her stockings sadly, that would be his undoing and it was. Deacon Robby Nobles snapped the picture! And took it right away to the officers of the Church.

The song selection of course was beautiful. One of Mira's favorites, Amazing Grace. As you have probably figured out by now the twenty six year old woman called Mira Sylvester, is a vital and very important person in my case. Her smile grew wide listening to her best friend Charmaine Lewis angelic voice move and enthrall the crowd to tears! All the church members with fans was swooning and waving them and sending their praises right up to God! The Holy Ghost was definitely in the building! Even Mira got to her feet praising the Lord! Charmaine from what I hear was born to sing! The petite Gospel Singer was known every Sunday to bring even the most unbreakable and strongest souls to their knees! Charmaine's voice traveled to every corner and every pew! Gaining new members every Sunday. Charmaine's father Daniel Lee Lewis was credited with having the good sense to let Toni Johnson, the Choir Director train the budding Songstress vocals to perfection. Daniel put in long hours down at Blink's Fix-It Shop just so's to see the fruit of his labor. And to afford his little princess, as well as his other children a proper upbringing. Daniel Lewis was a father of six. And had been working at the Fix-It Shop for over eighteen years!

Daniel wasn't a educated man. He took odd jobs here and there when need be. Any job really to cover the expenses for his family. Two hundred dollars every two weeks was nice chunk change, that brought a little piece of mind when they was very little. Today not so much. Elroy Albright was his boss. The hefty man used to snore loudly and very hard! And one of the highlights of Daniel's day was seeing him constantly fall out his chair! The good heart-ed seventy year old man laughed with him. "Someday this will be you!" he joked to the forty year old man. Daniel would help him up. "Not if I can help it sir!" More laughter form a friendship that was indeed becoming rock solid. So in return, Elroy made sure Daniel's kids wanted for nothing. He himself along with his pudgy chubby wife Amanda would buy those kids new clothes for Christmas. And at the start of every school year. The guy was lazy, but very nice. Besides he was smart enough to know that people talk. Daniel Lewis had just turned thirty five when he approached Elroy about a job. A man he would soon come to appreciate as a good friend. And who recently lost both his legs to diabetes. With very little resources, Mr. Daniel Lewis was still considered one of the smartest men in town! Six kids and the guy still went home to his wife.

Part 2

I walked the long narrow streets of Hopeful today. Hoping to find somebody who wasn't afraid to talk to me! And to tell me, what really went down at the Sienna Club the night Al Camelo was murdered. My partner Clara Jones was due to arrive on the next available flight out of Atlanta Georgia. It rained a lot in Hopeful, sure. But today the sun broke through, nice and sunny for a change. I was surprised to see some of the folks smiling and warming up to me. A lady sweeping her front porch gave me a kind wave. I checked the address. Yeah this was it, the Lewis residence. Mrs. Kady Lewis, Daniel's wife. Sat her broom aside seeing me approach. "Hello." she smiled warmly. We shook hands. She used to work at the airport when she was younger I was told. Nowadays she was a more reserved and soft spoken middle aged Clerk, working down at Hopeful's Bank And Trust. The guy who ran Omar's Bed and Breakfast where I grabbed the quick bite to eat this morning, gave me waffles and coffee on the house. His place was famous for their waffles. "Taste that sir!" he gleamed with pride. "Now I double dare you, tell me that, this ain't the best maple syrup you ever tasted!" I grinned a little deviously thinking about Clara downing that awfully stale hotel coffee, from a vending machine in a can!""Are you in town for long?" he asked. We don't get a lot of new faces up in here." I liked him he blended in well with small town living. "For as long as my Boss will keep me employed at the Prescient, I said. I'm originally from Stunson North Carolina." I tell him. " He adjusted his apron. "Oh yeah I know it? Real pretty up there, really nice. Most affluent black folks out there has a house on the hill. Is yours? "It is." I admit rubbing the back of my neck. But its also very quiet, except for the flocks of geese and all them birds in the yard! I couldn't stand it any longer! He laughed at that. "My parents love it! My father is a Used Car Salesman and my mother runs a Daycare. "Like I said, he repeated. Nothing but afflunt black folks!" he laughed heartily. I wasn't mad. "So you in town checking out the murder down at the Sienna Club. It was a statement. "Yeah, somebody's gotta do the dirty work.".. "Better you then me buddy." he said truthfully. "No offense.".." None taken. " I smiled. Like I said sir the food is on the house." Thank you." I kindly gestured as he walked away. "Oh and by the way!" He shouted running back to me after I finished my meal and was leaving. "Did you happen to talk to Kady yet?" I unclasped my notes checking the name. "Mrs. Lewis?".. "Yeah" he said barely meeting my eyes, Mrs. Lewis. " No I haven't." .."She used to be friends with Camelo's mother, Carlotta. They use to sing in the choir up at the church. Well anyways he coughed a bit, clearing his throat. Kady's very protective of her family and the lady's no fool!" So be warned! Just saying, don't underestimate her. Apparently there seemed to be ties between these two people. "We dated years back." he confirmed my suspicions. "She is a oxymoron at best tho!" he said reflective. "What do you mean?" I asked making way for a new customer. He gestured me to sit and removed his cap. "Because Mr. Miles, Kady is the type of woman who could cuss you out in a New York minute! But will never see you leave her house hungry!" His laugh rattled in his chest. And I suspected he was fighting a cold. "That's the kind of woman Mrs. Lewis has always been, he smiled. From the looks of him, I'd say he was still in love with her.

Thing is back in the day she was a plump and pleasing very intelligent dark skinned woman. And just as beautiful as her daughters. I read his tag. Samuel Higgins, he bent over dusting some crumbs off my table wiping at red spider veins under his eyes. I put his age at about late forties. Just go easy on the family is all I'm asking, is all." He tell me getting up to leave. "Sure." I committed before he walked away. I had finished my waffles and left the nice man a generous tip. Today January 9 2016 about a hour later, is when I met Mrs. Lewis. She excused herself for a moment to go put up her broom. She was a slender dark skinned woman now. Who seemed to be into physical fitness from the looks of her! She let me inside. They had a lovely home one to be proud of. "If you're talking about Mira Sylvester, she tells me. Motioning for me to sit. Of course I know her Detective! She's like one of my own daughters. So what do you want to know?" The woman eyes followed mines, over to her wall, where pictures of her children, her husband and even Mira hung. Along with I'm guessing other relatives inside well crafted wood and marble frames. "Mira was a little girl in one of those." She said to me, watching me staring at her photo giving me a knowing smile. That little girl use to run around on my porch sir and in and out my house with Charmaine tracking dirt to and fro! I suppressed a laugh at the way she said it. Mira was always bright eyed and loaded with intelligence even back then. "Won't you please sit Mr. Miles. The black leather sofa was spotless it looked brand new. But since the lady insisted, I did."Thank you very much." I sat staring at the tall woman moving around me in a long purple frock very loose fitting but very becoming. I used to chase those two around the room with a broom for messing up my shiny clean floors! she laughed. I was right, she was a neat freak! I'd shoo them away like the insects they were!" She lightly laughed again more dramatically this time! Hiding they were, right under my old rickety rackity sewing machine! she pointed! The one my mama left me. I threw it out last year. I think my mother would approve. The thing was a virtual rat trap! Full of cobwebs and dead spiders and such ewe! She stared at me in amazement. And yet? she stated. I would still call them back in the kitchen for a peppermint stick! The guy at the Bed and Breakfast was right about this woman, she was a oxymoron! "But I can tell you with a clear conscious Mr. Miles." She said taking a seat across from me. "Mira Sylvester would never kill anybody! Let alone Al Camelo. I've known them both for years." And right now my heart grieves for Carlotta so much." Her eyes watered over. I stood to leave. "Thank you very much ma'am." I shook her hand feeling better. "Nonsense! Sit back down and stay for dinner! Go on sit! Sit! I took a seat just in time to see Charmaine and Rufus coming through the door.

 Folks had no trouble giving me the low down on Daniel Lewis's. life. And how he used to tail chase on his lovely wife back in the day. I talked to a few of those women claiming him their baby daddy. "Lies!" his better half screamed at me setting place mats down on the table. I'm telling you sometimes I questioned my own sanity? Because I would swear beyond a reasonable doubt that this woman could be Diana Ross's twin! "He always comes homes for dinner detective always!" I could believe that my thoughts wandered. Whatever she was cooking, smelled so good! Charmaine was busy helping her mama prepare dinner. And intentionally ignoring me. Honestly? I think she was just curious and wondering why I was still there! And true to Mrs. Lewis's words, ol' Daniel Lee Lewis did showed up just in time for supper like the lady said. "Hey Kady baby!" He swung her around affectionately, in good spirits laughing. "I'm ready for another large slice of them ribs!" She was very wify to her husband." Daniel took his seat at the head of the table right after giving each of them a heart felt hugs. "Coming right up scrumptious!" she smiled at him. " And see I finished the chick peas, black eyed beans and sweet potato pie for you!" He stretched his neck up at her giving her a good ol fashioned smooch on the lips! "I know darling, I could smell them all the way down the street! And they smelled so good honey as always!" Was he over complimenting his lovely wife, because I was there? She bat those lashes at him enjoying his flirting. They was a mature couple. Who definitely was trying to keep the spark in their marriage. It was times like these that made me wish to settle down. Maybe with Mira or..Clara. I didn't know yet. I noticed Charmaine smiling at her parents, before putting all that good food on the table. "Of course your welcomed to have dinner with us Mr. Miles. by all means. Daniel stood wiping his hands on a napkin before shaking mine. Well I did catch Kady from the side of my eyes whispering in his ears. So logically it must have been about me. Charmaine had already set a extra plate, so how could I refuse. Maybe she did liked me just a little after all. One could only hope. (I smiled)

"Camelo had a lot of friends and a lot of enemies " Charmaine tells me breaking the ice between us. And the French bread placing it on my plate. She had seated herself next to me. "What about Mira, Charmaine?" I countered hitting the nail on the head. "She's a suspect in your old man's murder case you know." I've been told by a lot of people including your mother here in Hopeful I continued, that you two are friends. So, do you think she did it?" I'm sure she read the seriousness on my face accurately. Because that look on hers was so intense I almost choked on my peas! "I know you and her have a thing detective." She boldly states. I started writing taking her statement so's to avoid her penetrating glances. Obviously Charmaine shoots straight from the hip herself. "Camello liked her sister Payton, first. Before he dated me. They had a thing for a while. But she wouldn't give up the cookie." I choked on my drink! "Okay." was all I could say, wiping myself off. So they split up. Her head went down. But he has always favored Mira more. He made advances at her all the time. And on the day of his murder she was found in the back room where he usually fucked his whores." My pencil broke and everybody around the table stared at us in shock! I reached inside my pocket for a new one. And came eyeball to eyeball with Rufus, who seated himself on the other side of me. "What are you doing here Detective."he lazily drawled. I fixed my dark blue tie rising from my chair. "My job." I answered excusing myself. He pulled me by the tie bringing me closer to his face. Drawing attention from everyone else again. "Well your trail just ran cold detective!" I knock him off! "Who killed your boyfriend Charmaine!" I made one ditch last effort saying trying to clear Mira! "I have nothing more to say!" She yelled running pass me giving me the coldest look before storming upstairs! Charmaine's oldest brother Rufus in turn shoved me out the door! I stuck my notes back in the side pocket of my jacket. It had to be after nine o'clock when I walked to my car disgusted at the outcome! Cause all my leads right now, kept leading me no where! Rufus was a odd ball for sure. He looked like a nice guy but was far from it! Tall as he was, I heard he even played Basketball.

 I can't even lie, the kid did seem to evoke that certain something most Coaches look for in pro ballers. There was even talk of a Scout hanging around who had been in the stands for three weekends straight watching the games every Saturday. Or more to the point young Rufus himself! The family thought for sure Rufus was headed to the big leagues the crowning Mecca the NBA! Rufus displayed that certain pizzazz most Coaches like him go for. And it goes without saying his talent exceeded the guys expectation and never dissapointed! On Saturday what looked like the whole town turned out! And filled the stadium to capacity to watch Rufus play! The stadium sported the Mountain Cats, name in the middle of the field. All the way to the Sweetwater's main estate. Once Rufus even got famous enough in his hometown to earn a Sweetwater billboard from the old tycoon Vincent Sweetwater himself! Wesley Sweetwater was the oldest son of the Sweetwater clan and practically ran everything. They owned a huge chunk of Hopeful. Along with three other really prominent families. Camelo's family of course being one of them. Rufus helped the Hopeful Mountain Cats rip a new one in any opposing team, every Saturday all the way to the winning field goal! The dude got so use to being carried out on their shoulders it spoiled him! He had a nasty attitude now. And before long Daniel had spotted him talking with the Coach. I later learned that Rufus, was the reason for the big meal! And last but not least there was their middle sister Camay. The only musical Lewis who had joined the school band. The family was proud of all three of their older siblings! Tears well up in Daniels aging eyes thinking about those happier times. Camay surprised him! Here she was a sixteen year old budding beauty blowing a melodic tear jerkier so beautiful on such a simple stated instrument, the clarinet. She brought tears to his eyes! What a proud moment it had to be for her dad. Camey then did a instrumental solo of Somewhere Over The Rainbow with a boy who could make a tuba hum! Hopeful had some very talented kids! "Wow" Daniel sniffed removing his cap in respect after they finished, fighting back manly tears. Daniel had a well spring of talent in his family and a reason to be forever grateful.

The three youngest siblings Daniel Jr. Lucy Louise and tiny Ruby Ray Lewis had yet to show what skills they possessed. But this write up is about a murder. One that involved Lewis's three older children Rufus, Charmaine and Camay. And of course Mira. Everybody from the parking lot to the stands fell under the spell that was Camay. Enjoying his lovely daughter's etheral tunes. Daniel moved closer staring at her feeling extra proud! She reminded him of himself. He played a instrument! His famous harmonica. If you needed a entertainer for the evening, for events such as birthdays and weddings. Then he was your man. His treasured harmonica was always available. Years later it now lay rusting inside a golden case gathering dust. He was hoping to pass it down to Daniel Jr. but the boy was only six. I was told that Rufus had developed the big head from all the adulation the good citizens of Hopeful heaped upon him and they was right! He then began considering himself too good for the slow developing mining town. A town he considered stagnant to progress! Oh sure the Sweetwaters was given credit for moving the sleepy little town into the 21 century! And the Sienna was Hopeful's heartbeat! Other than that it was lazy. CEO Wesley Sweetwater had connections all over the country! But not even that impressed Rufus Lewis.

Part 3

The Sweetwaters was the first family in Hopeful. Their ancestors settled the rural mining town. That's right, you read it right. Black folks, settled the place, that a lot of white people found disgusting. But the Sweetwaters fixed it up! The mine yielded diamonds as well as gold. Nobody in their right mind would step foot inside that snake infested cave! But they did. And lost very few casualties. Once a gusher of crude oil shot up! Turning the family into instant millionaires! It goes without saying that Rufus did at least, held a lot of respect for the Sweetwaters. He wanted the good life like them! And wanted it now! And thought the only other progressive thing about the city was the drug dealers! Sadly he even considered that progress! A knot laid up against his father's head today, and was getting larger. It was the reason Daniel wore a cap to dinner. He never let on to his dear wife that he'd been mugged and beaten pretty severely. Daniel must have some really good friends. Because they cleaned him up quite nicely! No doubt Coffee had put it there! "Son come on..he said. Calling Rufus from among them. Yo mama will be getting worried. Come on na, lets go home." Coffee spit out a laugh. "Damn it! Just git your ass outta my face already old man! What part of your boy belonging to the streets you don't understand?! That was followed by kicking dirt in the man's face! Git it now padna! But if you gonna have a problem with that" The old man of seventy years old took four hard kicks to the groin this time doubling over, before buckling to his knees! And then a hard butt, from Coffee's gun! Coffee had always solved his shit with fighting! He stood around them laughing with his boys. All Daniel could see was his son standing there with them saying nothing! Daniel then slowly picked up his hat dusting it off walking away. What else could he do? The streets had him now! Feeling like a broken man spitting up blood in front of his son. Lewis mumbled to himself ignoring their rude remarks. Mr. Lewis removed the liquor bottle out of his pants pocket uncapping it, frowning over at them. He took a long swig before wiping his graying beard dragging himself home.

"Are you sure you went to the airport Wes? Please tell me Sweetwater Corporation, is as clean as the water your family's pumping into this community?" Wes stared over at his incredibly beautiful wife Payton snickering, before sitting his suitcase down. He'd just walked through the door and was cold, wet and shivering. The fireplace was going, it felt nice. He could've sworn he heard her talking on the phone when he walked in. She looked worried she was always worried. "I was talking to my mother." She admit reading his expression correctly."We're clean Payton okay..satisfied? And yes I heard about Camelo's death while waiting on my flight. So I got back here as soon as possible." He took her in his arms, from routine not affection. Giving her a kiss so brief if you blink, you'll miss it. She trembled against him. Staring up at him wondering if just for once her husband was being sincere. "I was also talking to my sister Mira on the phone." She informed him. "She's over by our mother. She told me Camelo's brother Marco was also at the Sienna Club last night. Did you know that honey? She saw him and Camelo go upstairs to Camelo's office".." So?" he said wryly, dismissing her altogether removing his wet jacket, taking a seat by the fireplace. Wasn't Marco supposed to be in China last night with you? Overseeing your capital investments. And then after that, meeting with some of Vincent Sweetwater's new clients at the Hiyak?" Your father went their yesterday. Wesley hated his wife's inquisitive nature. It was broads like her that turned a man gray early! "Babe I said, relax okay. he shook his head, feeling tired. Marco is still in China as we speak, Payton. I talked to him myself. Besides your sister will lie about anybody and anything at this point!" Isn't she a suspect? he laughed. Payton turned away wringing her hands. "That's not funny Wes." He got up and went kissed her on the cheek. "But accurate, right doll face!"

Look, I said she was mistaken alright? Marco ain't due back here until sometime tonight, he stated, with sex hungry eyes staring at their curvy maid Keke. She brought him a drink. And Payton did not miss the little flirtation between the two. But refused to say anything more until she left. "This is a small town darling and people talk." Marco is banging the Sienna Club's piano player Mr. Dalton, did you know that Wes?" That's what huh? She counted on her fingers. His fourth gay lover this week." Wes sipped his drink answering dryly. "That ain't our business." I believe Mira is innocent Wes, she pushed her point. Why would she lie? " There was a long silence. "Wesley if you had Camelo killed, I swear I'd leave your ass so fast!" His eyes twitched. Wesley shot straight up angrily throwing his empty glass in the clean furnace breaking it! Marching towards her. "And there it is!" His laughter was slime! He tossed his hands up, feeling vindicated! "You kept dismissing what I said and could see with my own eyes! Is it my imagination now Payton! Every time I caught him flirting with you! You said it was nothing! So now you finally ready to admit the truth to me! " Sit down you clown, you're drunk! He was laughing. What is wrong with you! Payton breathed hotly! She couldn't believe he was up in here airing out their dirty laundry in front of their employees! "Don't worry slut! I ain't laid hands on your man! But don't you push me Payton Sweetwater, not tonight!" You really are starting to forget your place around here! "Oh you mean the part where we, ain't nothing but window dressing in this generic town of Hopeful?! Believe me I'm more than aware! She stretched those light brown eyes! They are so eager to see a rich loving black couple holding it down! Yay! Black love right baby! While we fall short! And is so far from it!" She stood balding up her fist, yanking on her botched green dress looking upstairs, hoping the children wasn't in ear shot! So much frustration was coming outof both of them! Why? Was this really their way of grieving of Camelo?

"You seem to keep forgetting my dear wife he pressed! That I didn't marry you for love. But out of obligation!" He said it, grinding those words in his mouth with a hatred she could see! Making her nervous. "Come on baby, don't go getting delusional on me now Payton!" Wes had always knew how to push her buttons! And yes right now, she was more than angry with him! Why are we having such a discreet conversation out in the open like this huh? Instead of behind closed doors! Sadly it was already too late for either of them to stop now! Otherwise Payton could be so sweet and discerning, something she learned to be in that house! She was breathing hard now, trying her best to hush him! "Alright Wesley I get the point! Look just shut up alright! And please lower your damn voice! The kids is sleeping upstairs! Eight years and three kids with you! And you still don't love me! "Why can't you just move on? she tells him seriously. Its obvious Clara has!" She regretted saying it the moment she saw his face! "Keep her name out your got damn mouth you hear me!" he warned, this time really scaring her! And if that wasn't enough she saw the maids Keke and Julia peeping. They came out pretending to be doing house work. Payton stared over at the broken glass on the floor by the fireplace annoyed. Keke went over to tidy up. Sweeping until everything was spotless again. Both maids ignored her like they always do, when Wesley came home. "No..you're right Wes. She took a deep breath saying.

We did not marry for love!" And no, we do not have a ideal marriage either. She boldly admit in front all of them. Like they didn't already know! "And if you hadn't put a baby in me, a virgin! Maybe your daddy the Lord and Master of all Hopeful, wouldn't have stopped your wedding to Clara Jones!" Wesley yanked poor Payton off her feet! He swung her around by the arm pretty roughly until she yield! She shoved him off her! Losing her balance, before hitting the floor! To his credit Wesley did try to catch her. "Why do I even try to love you?" she shook her head miserably, up at him disgusted. You're so mean to me, you has always been mean to me. "Payton sniffed, getting up off the shiny panel wood flooring heading for the stairs." I still love Clara, Payton. I never lied to you about it!" No you didn't, but god I really wished you did." She turn up her lips finally feeling foolish."Thing is I spotted the gold digger in you too late! You didn't want me Payton or loved me! You just wanted my money! he holler behind her. Trying to console himself with a lie. Because your family was dirt poor! All you girls had going for you was your looks!. Keke reached him another drink, smiling. It was that way in the beginning Wes. But I did fall in love with you. Stop lying to my face girl! He said watching her mount the stairs. "You just like your mama and your sister Payton! He yell from the rails.."Y'all ain't nothing but a bunch of hoes preying on rich men!".. "Like your mother!" She shot back! Payton toss her drink on him from where she stood and made sure some of it hit Keke! And by the way darling" he scoffs wiping himself off with a silk hanky. "Don't you ever forget I know the real reason you refused to take that paternity test?" My oldest son Roman is starting to look more and more like Camelo!"

She counted five servants peeping at them now but didn't care! They wanted to be all up in rich folks business? Then she won't hold nothing back! She'll give this community a show they will talk about for years! "You bastard! And did you kill him for thinking that stupid shit!" Payton exploded ignoring his advances towards her! Wes passed her, heading to Roman's bedroom! "She threw her arms open blocking his way! Stop! Stop it Wes! "He's yours you dummy! She hoarsely say, so pissed she was losing her sanity! You both have the same birth mark go check! He did, turning his sleepy son, carefully trying not to wake him. It was on the boy's lower back, the same as his. "Is that proof enough for you idiot!".. Camelo and me went out a couple of times! He wanted sex right out the gate! I broke p with him! He had that shit for a bad habit! Wanting to fuck not talk! But you know what? Maybe I should have fucked him instead of you! "Keep pushing me Payton you here me! He seethed. Keep pushing and watch me file for divorce and get it! Her golden colored cheeks flushed. And her curly black hair loss some of the bounce it had on her shoulders. Payton's mascara was even gone. Come to think of it, she was more a fairer version of Mira. Who was reddish brown. Payton overheard everything said downstairs. Why not, nobody in that house had any respect for her anyways! Eight years and nothing to show." she quietly say to him. "Except our children." Wes wiped his face, look just go..go to bed!" We'll talk more calmer in the morning! He was staring at his son, not her. "Tomorrow, I'm leaving you." She opened her son's door and left out. "Payton!" Wes called after her. Payton! Shit then whatever!" Payton went laid across their own bed listening to female voices and her husband, leaving out the door. No doubt later on, he'd would be occupying one of the guest rooms but not alone. She grabbed her cell phone with her hands shaking, fumbling it a bit. "Hey Mira, yeah its me. There was a long pause on the other end. "You think you can put me and the kids up for about a week? I'm leaving him, I leaving Wes.."..Really? She hear her sister say relived. Well, its bout time." Mira sat up in bed, yawning fixing her head wrap, wiping sleep out her eyes. "And of course you can, stay as long as you like." Thank you sis!" Payton said relieved herself. She then proceed to wake up all three of her children and took down their coats. It was dark enough for them to leave in their pj's. They sneaked out getting in the car. Payton had took one last look around downstairs, before leaving the house keys inside the fireplace. And leaving Wes for good!

Chapter 4

 My typewriter ran out ink. So I got up to replace it. The sleep derpervation by now had long since kicked in. I lit my fifth cigarette for the night. Then poured a little Brandy in my wine glass, straight no chaser. God my eyelids was heavy as hell! How long had I been working here? It felt like months. "I could use some fresh air." I got up walking over to the window. "Great" The howls and smell of dog greeted my irritated sinus after lifting the balcony window. I shoved the latch shut. Ain't nobody had time for that! Besides the only other thing coming in was cold air. So I went sit back down. It was still dark out. "No rest for the weary I tell myself. My eyes then traveled to the phone. "Still no calls." I mumbled the words out loud, wondering where Clara was. Ain't no way she was home sleep in her bed unless it was the crack of dawn! I cracked a smile thinking about her. Hell she was more a sleuth then I was! "There I had said it." But not to her, never to her! I laughed at my own asinine joke bobbing my cigarette up and down off the side of my chin grinning. I felt like one of those old guys in an old classic movie. I was Bogart and Clara was Lauren Bacall. She'd fix that and make us Foxy Brown and Gavin (pretty boy) Marchand whatever. The woman was a dog in heat when she caught scent of a lead! And woe be it unto any man or woman that crossed her path! "I laughed again enjoying my silliness oh god I was really pathetic. And god only knows what Clara would do to me if she hear any of this stuff! Shit I'd never live it down!

I do remember the Chief saying, Ms. Clara Jones had sniffed us out a new bone. Meaning a lead! Call me crazy, but I missed smelling that woman's minty fresh breath all up in my face early in the morning and in my mouth. We be doing fine, until I bring up Mira. Then some mythical banshee in the form of Clara takes over attacking my ribs! My cell went off! "Hey now!." I danced trying to twerk! Damn man my ringtone of Snoop's Gin and Juice still sounded good! And thank god too because I was starting to go bat shit crazy up in here! "Holy cow!" I leap up yelling almost spilling the contents of my drink. "The fuck Clara way to come for my ghost!" She was standing in my doorway shaking out her wet hat! "What I sacred you?" she was laughing. God she had been quieter then a mouse! She must have used the spare key I gave her after three weeks of incredible sex! Or otherwise I was getting careless."Hey good looking you miss me?"she said coming all the way in. "Oh and by the way, you should get that, its the boss." Or maybe Mira!" I tried it and yes I was the lowest of the low. But Clara surprised me! She was holding that African banshee in check! "Never mind she poke her tongue at me, I'll get it myself! Of course she walked by shoving me by the head. Alright...scratch the banshee holding in part."Hey Mus-turd yeah he's still up." The Chief rubbed his entire face agitated. "Very funny Clara, and its Mustard!" I know, she grinned. I smiled taking the phone from her. "What's up boss? Clara was switching on lights. Killing the last receptical keeping my eyes awake.

She reached me her cleaning bill. That's right the woman was a clean freak! Apparently the rain and fox fur didn't mix. Clara pursed those bow lips! It has been raining the entire day. Just like the news said! But it was a moot point starting an argument with Clara about all thing the weather! "Yeah like I control the weather Clara give me a break!" I finally said. "Right" she stuck the bill in my pocket. "Now if you two is finished, maybe we can get down to work! "Meh." the lady tossed her head at us taking a seat. "I just received a message from the FBI you two. They want you to go and talk to what's her name?" "I let out a deep breath. "Mira?" Yeah that's who! "I also got word that you been burning the candle on both ends of the stick tonight Slick?"..I stared around dumbfounded. "From who?" Your housekeeper, she's under cover. "Great" I stretched the word as Clara laughed. She then took a puff off my dwindling cigarette."Yes detective my love we are not working alone." Clara shoved the cigarette though my teeth shutting my mouth. She knew I didn't like no third party, we was enough! What about you Clara?" Did you know about the FBI involvement? I asked the silly question knowing full well she was gonna lie. My lips even traveled up the corners waiting on the lie. It did felt good to hear her voice after such a long grueling day.

"Yes I did." she lied. I always check my messages. I could always tell when she was lying. I gave Clara one of my crooked smiles, that said..yeah right. She smiled back. God we just knew each other too well. I took the phone from her putting it on speaker phone." Well Chief I found out the old man went confront Coffee like a damn fool." I tell him. Yeah I saw it just now in your report Clara offered. She was reading. "I see Coffee's territory is mostly all of Monroe St. now. That's on the edge of town Miles. Man Lewis got a lot of balls going there I give him that! Ain't nothing out there but old grave yards where trucks go to die. That's right Clara and its not called dope alley for nothing." I interrupted. Damn those large cow eyes on that woman had the audacity to be surrounded by the longest and prettiest lashes I'd ever seen! Either I was tired as hell at this point, or Clara Jones was beginning to look like a snack! "She went in for the kiss I was thinking about giving her. "Miles I think Mr. Lewis was angry because Coffee started recruiting too close to his old friend's house and messing with his son. She breathe hot and sexy all over me, sending that mint flavor breath down my throat. "No doubt I agreed. Its why they sent the younger kids to live with their auntie in Richmond Virginia. Until the shit blows over. We pressed that kiss home! "He probably told Coffee to stay away from Rufus. she said or rather threatened him. "Sure." And that beating was the result." We was trying to fly under the radar cause the boss was listening. But she was soaking wet and teasing the corners of my mouth. "Clara five bucks says they already got to Rufus." Clara got on her tipsy toes. It felt unreal having her long snake like tongue sucking mine! We was all over each other! Mustard on the other hand had been listening and catching a fit on the other end! "Fuck you!" He blew a fuse! Are you guys gonna work? Or get a fucking room!"..."Get a room." we both laughed as Clara pulled a face. "Oh Musturd your such a mood killer! We haven't seen each other all day."

"Look did I hire a couple of grown ups here! Or a pair of hormonal teens! Because if the latter is true? Its never too late for me to pull your sorry asses off this mutha fucka!" I cleared my throat and put some distance between me and the cookie dough known as Clara Jones! Cause that nigga was talking borderline crazy right about now! He was messing with my money! I had invested way too much time and foot power stepping over shit grenades laying in my way! For him to start talking pulling the plug on us now! Even Clara for buckled under pressure and almost fainted feeling for the sofa! The poor thing almost looked anemic! ! You can mess with our heads but never with our money! That was the slogan we lived by. "Do I have your attention NOW detectives!" he roared like a lion. "Yes sir!..Yes Chief! We both say feeling the heat from that ghastly blow hard! Alright then! Clara, tell Detective Prescott what you found out about um,..ur...damn what's her name again?" I could've strangled him! "Mira doofus!"..."Whatever." he blow it off like a child. "Right now, she's our number one prime suspect after Rufus Lewis." I wanted to be more sensitive with this case Miles, Clara spoke up. Because of your involvement with her. So I made sure all the witnesses statements was legit. That's what took me so long. "Finally the truth." I said as she darted those pretty brown eyes away,nervously. I wasn't born yesterday. Clara pretended well. But that pact we made last year about having a open relationship, right now? Seemed to be a bad idea on her part I guess, not mine. Clara looked hurt. She said she was fine with me and Mira hooking up. And yet... I wanted to believe her! "Say something Miles." she whispered close to my ear, interrupting my thoughts. I couldn't. Did she wanted me to lie and say this was only a fling? There's no way I could that! I respected her too much for that! I could only let silence sweep through us, leaving her bruised emotions hanging for now without an answer. "To answer your question about Rufus, Clara. I said side stepping our situation. And after hearing our boss's dragon spirit animal breathing fire under his breath. "Go on darling" she urged sniffing a little..damn. "Rufus did went to see Coffee. That much we do know." She redid her lipstick turning her back to me. When she faced me again, she was back in detective mode.

"Are you saying that Rufus has joined the mob already? What happened with his sweet deal to go to the NBA?" She took a seat staring at my empty whiskey glass. Both the boss and I say "scraped." How come?" The boss this time went quiet. Because of his sister Camay. "What about Camay, Chief?" I sat next to her but she slid down leaving a lot of space between us. "Camay was involved in a nasty car accident at the beginning of the year. He checked his reports. "January 3 2016 to be precise. Her car was driven off the road and over a cliff by a unmarked vehicle. Luckily she survived. "I gather the accident was no accident?" Clara went fixed herself a drink. "You got it, not by a long shot." he said resealing the report. You interested in knowing why Clara? Of course go on." she sip. Because it happened the same day Rufus was expected to sign with the NBA. Coincidence? I think not. "Rufus instead felt obligated to his family. So he took his younger sister to the hospital instead. We got a witness saying, the man could never stand by and watch his mama cry. It cost him...big. The Scout signed German Nolan, the guy staring in all those gym wear commercials now. "That's rough" Clara say up at me. I smiled. "The guys career was over before it started huh?" I crossed the room saying sitting next to her again, she got up.

"Daniel's son Rufus, had been approached by Camelo's goons long before the accident. That's why this shit smelled to high heaven and stronger then the turd Coffee got himself into. Are you saying you suspect whatever happened with Camay ties directly in with Camelo's murder Chief? "Yes I am." And you know as well as I do Wesley Sweetwater couldn't afford another family scandal after what went down nine years ago. Or another family taking their place as the richest family in Hopeful. And that's exactly what Rufus would have made his family. "Why bring Wesley into this Chief? Clara stood surprisingly obviously taking offense."Why not Wesley, Clara." Mustard held his ground, knowing full well he would get a rise out of her. Since the boss seemed to have left me completely out of the conversation, I went fix myself something to eat. I was no chef far from it. But my left over stakes smothered in a mushroom sauce sure tasted pretty good to me. The chief held his nose, but I paid the simp no mind shit the food was good!

"And by the way Miles, Camelo's older brother Marco took a flight out suddenly that night also. I stared because I was busy garbling my words and my food. And we was also informed that Rufus sister Charmaine was spotted with him at the airport. Pretty fishy don't you think? She got on the plane with him? Sure did. "Are you talking the night Camelo was murdered Chief?" he nods. It was Clara's turn this time to be surprised. My tip followed them to a motel she reported that Charmaine was laid up in there with him all night. Had to be cause she never saw her leave. But they both took separate flights back here the next day. "My god how deep is this shit? Clara say to me forgetting we weren't talking. "Deep." I replied following my forkful with some wine. And get this? Are you paying attention Miles?

The Chief said turning pages. I bit my tongue before saying yes." I noticed Clara's hand had started shaking. She was so upset she reached for my pack of cigarettes lighting up. "Wes and I got history of which you are well aware of Chief. Don't you dare go down that road and don't make Wes part of this sick investigation." I hated to play devil's advocate against Clara, but Mira's life was on the line here and I do mean...literally. "I know you two was engaged Clara that's public record. And you left him at the alter." Because that arrogant Vincent Sweetwater wouldn't let his golden boy marry a Police woman."Fuck you Miles! she slapped my face! " Nice detective. The Chief winced dragging the words shaking his head. Damn man! Have you ever heard of tact? he stressed. Clara was wiping tears now. "Next time just go for the jugular Miles and save yourself some time!" I tried holding her. "No get off me!" she shouted anger shoving me away.

"Don't buckle on me now partner! I grabbed her before she reached the door. Not when I need you Clara! Do you need me Miles? Do you really? Bullshit! Why did it feel like those words also smacked me across the face! And why everything I tried to do to bridge the gap between us kept falling apart! Let go of me! ..she pleaded shoving at me harder. I held on wondering why I couldn't let go! The Chief stood up watching us. Did I make Clara feel insecure? "I said move! So what do you want me to do huh Miles? Do you want to shield a murderer for you! Is that it? "tears shined in her eyes. "That's cold Clara." I said finally turning her loose. "Now let me ask you a question okay? Which one are we talking here, Mira or Wesley?" She balled her mouth at me and slapped me harder! Damn Clara I'm going to need surgery! "I'm way pass tired of your bullshit! I'll talk to you tomorrow Chief." The Chief nods with his eyes on me. Clara slammed the door this time almost off the hinges! Yeah she was that mad...wow! And that made me feel some type of way. The Chief was drumming a pencil on his desk barely looking at me. "You know Miles I wasn't going to bring up the Sweetwaters in front of Clara. That was insensitive on my part. I knew it'll be a sore spot for her. Not just because of Wesley my old friend, but because of you too. I just can't play tippy toes around the case no more! Not when we're on the verge of a break through! "I feel you." We both sit. "Look." The Chief said. "I may be aging like a pit bull but come on nigga! You know you and Clara are way more than just friends! Shit the entire police force know! Miles I don't know what your intentions are with these two women. And before you say anything, I realize its none of my business okay. But I have known Clara a long time. Nigga..she don't deserve this!" He held up a hand because I opened my mouth. "You better decide something real soon. I lit up and didn't day anything until I exhaled.

"Garner you remember me telling you that when Clara and I started this relationship that it was her decision for us to have a open one, no strings attached she said. You remember that, right?." .."I do" the Chief lit a cigar. "Then isn't it ironic she wanted the damn thing when I didn't! If she couldn't handle seeing me with another woman? Shit forget it! The Chief pat my back. I never wanted to hurt her! I raked my hands through my hair saying staring at the man for some answers. The Chief went got his hat and put it on his head. "She sounds like a woman in love to me! Man I hate getting caught up in other people's affairs. Good night Miles." He pat my shoulder leaving. "Nite Chief." I had been dismissed by the woman I'd been sleeping with for eight years! "And all I kept hearing from her was Mira had been left alone with Camelo's body in the back room for some time. They even have her on surveillance tape along with Rufus climbing out the window! Shit how can I even fuck with that! What kind of evidence could I produce to prove her innocence against such damaging shit! My head pounded! I wasn't just mad I was angry! I kicked over my chair so hard I bruised my big toe! Clara's case was air tight against Mira! "Still I had been in this business far too long to know that shit could sometimes smell like sugar." Camelo had a lot of enemies! If I was going to turn this case around, I had to start from there. The lines has been drawn between partners and... lovers.

Part 5

So much has happened since me and Clara started this case. But Mira would never suspect Clara being bold enough to knock on her door. Mira answered sucking in breath. "What do you want? Clara showed her her badge walking pass her into the room. Or should I say used her badge. "I'm not here to mince words with you, Mira. I don't like you and I'm sure you don't like me. So since we've got that out of the way. I need to get on a more personal note with you. "Okay, I'll bite." What are you trying to be to Miles, just a girlfriend or a wife? I'm asking this seriously. Mira shut her door after seeing people coming. "Drink?" No thanks. Clara said staring around the place just as impressed as I was. The woman was living lavish. Somehow she knew the answer to the question in her head, Camelo. Mira poured herself a drink. She wasn't dressed whorish but had on a nice pair of sweats, obviously she was working out. "Miles is the only man in my life. And yes Clara, I'm hoping to keep that way. Clara almost took a seat. Her words left her winded. Well did it ever accured to you, that you wasn't the only woman in his? Mira stare at her. I'm twenty five and you are what twenty eight? "Twenty nine." Clara corrected her. Mira did sit. And are you telling me you haven't figured out men yet? They always have side piece. And wish is you Mira? I can ask you the same Clara. Yo know my mother had a old saying. Two mountains will never meet, but two women will. I guess she was right. I am the woman he right now needs in his life. But with Miles I'm not afraid to admit to you, that this could easily turn to love. Clara scoffed, hating Mira even more. But at least she didn't mince words or deny anything. "What..you think you can slobber his knob better than me?" was Clara's best defense. Mira stood up. "Well he's still with me. What does that tell you?" I did a quickie knock at Mira's door letting myself in. "Clara?" I said astonished finding her there. She walked right up to me and slapped me hard! Before walking out. "Now what was that for?!" I rubbed my stinging cheek saying after her, before turning to Mira. "I don't know." she shrugs her shoulders..smiling.

(The next day)

"Wes is clean Miles leave me alone." Clara blocked my cell after that, clicking her line dead. Rufus knew his daddy wouldn't let it slide after Coffee paid a visit to their home and beat him up in their back yard. That happened two days before the murder. Rufus was okay thinking about becoming a Gangster until the reality of actually being one presented itself. "I just want to play ball man that's all" he blubbered holding his gut. His nose streamed blood so heavy he swallowed some. "Why you working for Camelo again Coffee?" Rufus attempt to ask risking getting punched in the eye! Shut the fuck up! Coffee socked him in it. His eye swelled and quickly blackened. I ask the questions around here Mr. Ivy League! Next time I'll do more than put that eye out, you'll loose some teeth! All Rufus knew right now was that it was hard to breath. "I'll give you a cut of whatever money they offer me man..damn it I promise, Just..just keep my family out of this nigga! "He was begging for their lives detective instead of his own." The next door neighbor was telling us, word for word of what he overheard that morning. Clara stared every where but at me. I was shocked really that she even showed up it was good to see her. I reached her the statements from the other neighbor. She was standing behind me all professional like ignoring me while doing her job. For now we had formed a truce and I was fine with that. As long as we got paid, she would have laughed. Clara studied the information quietly saying nothing.

"That's when I heard Coffee promised to rape Ms. Charmaine! Saying you know I'm partial to chocolate, what her fine self! He and his goons started laughing sickening!" Clara's head shot up! "What!" I was surprised too. "Oh its no secret around here, that Coffee was sweet on the girl! He has been for years. Hearing somebody talk about his sister like man, he say to me. I shook my head understanding. "Were they lovers?" Clara asked point blank Charmaine and Coffee."To be honest detectives, he breathed through the words, I don't really know. "It was Rufus who stopped Mira

Sylvester from getting gang raped by some boys in high school. After that he would walk those two girls to school. He may look bad detectives but Rufus really ain't. "Clara's eyes fell in mine, was that a subtle hint she was giving me, or a emotional response? He relay us all the sordid details. "I have to ask sir, I know Charmaine was raised, because of her Christian upbringing. But what about Mira, was she a tease? I knew those words was meant to hurt me, to sting. "Not at all!" he admitted taken aback. That girl's only problem was the fact that a lot of boys found her cute and that ain't her fault now is it miss? "No it isn't." I agreed. Please continue sir? I tell him. "Well Rufus been with a few girls, here and there, his crush tho was Mira. I hear his recent girlfriend is that pretty lil Betty Creesy. Well that is, until old man Vincent Sweetwater took a liking to her. She worked with Ms. Mira, down at the Sienna Club. Too bad they closed the place leaving all those people unemployed. "You seen Betty have ya detective? he cackled showing missing teeth. That Betty is a real looker!" He coughed, winking over at Clara. "And you ain't too bad yourself Ms. Detective." he winked again. Clara was looking at me instead of him. Oh she knew I had to be smiling like a chest cat inside.

She could see it from the hint of a smile on my face! "And she's single." I tell him." Is that right." the old man said pulling on the long salt and pepper beard on his chin, checking Clara more closely. She walked ahead of us fuming as he lead us to his front door. "We got some mighty pretty women here in Hopeful..huh detective? I nod at him agreeing behind Clara's back."Coffee punched that boy several times over there Detectives, after putting his face in that concrete wall. I think he cracked Rufus nose. "I want my money! he was yelling. "Now git the fuck outta here before I put a bullet in your ass crack sweet boy!" Coffee really has become the lowest of the low." The old guy was shaking his head sadly. He ain't always been that way you know. Only got like that since his parents was killed in that flood back in 06. That changed the boy. For young men, both him and Rufus sure have aged a lot! They look older. And both them boys is only twenty seven years old! "Clara stared at me as if agreeing with the old guy's assessment. "How old are you detective, if you don't mind my asking? "Thirty two. "I remember thirty two he smiled at me kinda wickedly. "Go on sir." Clara said still taking notes. "Well Miss. Lady, ol Rufus ran after Coffee yanking his gun out his back pocket!" Coffee liked to pissed his pants! he laughed shoving me. Then I was surprised to hear Rufus say, "You got a deal okay?" I'll do what you ask, just leave my damn family alone! He was breathing hard holding his ribs when he said it. Rufus then tossed Coffee back his gun. "You betta." Coffee blew that off staring at him really hard before taking off in his Range Rover.

 "Here's the other Neighbor's statement Chief." I handed it to him back at the station. The boss had been quiet up until now. Eye deep in the papers in front him. But at least he was finally impressed with our work. He gave us both thumbs up before taking a seat. "So I gather that's why Rufus didn't do anything when they beat up his old man in front him, sad." That's right, Coffee wanted his piece of Rufus and he got it. I agreed. You know boss me and Clara sent Coffee and Cobra to jail for smuggling coke into the Sienna Club four years ago. I know Miles I ain't forgot. So why would Camelo hire him back? "He didn't." Clara butt in. "His brother Marco did." The Chief expelled breath.. " That's right." Cole Banks aka Coffee would never pass up the chance to slither his ass back into Marco's good graces. The Sienna Club was willed to Marco. Because of Marco's blood ties with the Sweetwaters. You see Marco thought if he stuck close to that family he'd get rich! He didn't want the Sienna, it wasn't competitive enough for him, to make him a quick millionaire! He later learned he was wrong. He stupidly gave it to Camelo. Little did he know ha, it would end up making Camelo a very rich man. Marco has always been the Sweetwaters right hand man ever since they cleaned him up and gave him a job. Just a glorified yes man,really. Clara added taking a seat on the end of his desk. They never paid him the amount of money he hoped for, that's right Clara. The Sienna Club was the real gold mine, he discovered too late. You ever been to the Forest Lake Condo Apt Miles? Nothing but the rich in Hopeful resides there. Marco lives there too and so does Mira as you already know. Clara stared at me.

Anyways we found out Marco is only renting! But Camelo owns two elaborate homes past the forest and the one Mira's living in. Its a resident area he could never afford.

"We all know Camelo turned the Sienna into a drug paradise detectives, that's old news! And Rufus? Was their golden goose that would keep them on easy street!" The NBA money." Clara put in. "That's right, give the lady a cigar." she nods. It ain't no surprise to me Camelo turned up dead detectives to be honest." The chief admit locking back his files. "And it didn't hurt Cole none to hear the boy was very vocal about leaving Hopeful for the good life! Rufus craved the big city! So if he gave them what they wanted. He figured they would give him what he wanted." That NBA check meant everything to all of them, I finished that thought. "And they would have Rufus throw his entire family under the bus to get it!" Clara rolled her eyes."Sorry boys" But I'm going to have to throw a monkey wrench in your nice neat little package. This is a crime of passion and nothing else!" A woman did this. Well I got a brawl uptown to stop so I'll leave you two to work this out." The Chief shook my hand and gave Clara a friendly peck on the cheek before shutting the door behind him. "I'm right you know." Clara say after I locked it. "Well we can't say for sure Clara right now its all circumstantial evidence. I rolled the dice at her, she didn't pick up. "Miles ..Camelo was stabbed with a stake knife! "I'm going on record saying a woman did it!" She sat crossing her long legs lady-like lighting up.

I could tell this was a case Clara wished I'd worked alone. She watched me pace the floor. My black robe was hanging open I was unaware. Letting her dark eyes feast on the mouth full she was used to. God only knows why I wore briefs in the first place I'm a damn single man and normally walked around butt naked! Her lips parted. And I wanted to slip my tongue between them it had been a long time. Her full juicy lips gave me a massive hard on. God they was huge, supple and juicy! Large enough to suck a man straight to heaven! "So you're telling me Coffee filled Rufus head with even more nonsense." She said in that trance of hers fixated on my prick." I went poured whiskey down my throat, I needed it! "Yeah" I tell her trying not to lose it! He gassed Rufus head up good. She came over to where I was. Her perfume reaching me first. Lord why Clara had to be so bold! "Miles you know Coffee would claim the kid eventually. That's how the mob works. She intertwined a long shapely leg between mine. It was hairless like the pussy I was rubbing. How convenient no underwear. Leaving my hungry eyes no choice but to gaze pass her plunging neckline. Clara had the type of huge boobs that sat up at attention. All silky smooth with a light powder dusting fragrance, the color of her skin! They would make a plastic surgeon jealous. She undid some buttons I undo the rest. "So now he's working for the mob? She asked leaning into me working her lower body in a circular motion then up and down, just pleading for me to go down. God I thought I was gonna spill right there! She stare me in the eyes satisfied with my reaction, giving me a wicked grin. I used that opportunity to slip my tongue between those massive wet full lips finally. "You want me?' she teased rubbing me making me larger. "Tell me how much you want me Miles." I had her black slip up around her hips, pressing my answer home down there. Jesus Clara don't make me beg for it! "Oh wait that's right, she startled me saying. I'm not Mira! She playfully pushed me away. Finish yourself off idiot!" Or call your precious girlfriend! I fell back on my knees rolling around on the floor aching for release! A release that I eventually would.. took care of myself!

chapter 6

The following day)

" I heard they was a close knit family, the Lewis family I mean." Clara was still digging for clues in my file drawer that could still seal my girlfriend's fate. "Sorry abot last night." I left out shaking my head. As I walked down the long corridors to the chief's office, I heard footsteps coming up fast behind me.

"Prescott!" I turned on my heel to find Vincent Sweetwater baring those yellowing dentures of his too early in the morning. "I been meaning to catch up with you detective. To give you and the lady detective the praise you deserve! "That sounded odd. "Why?" We ain't solved the case yet." He had a rough sounding voice and very deep. And also the smile of a crocodile. I just needed to know why the two of you dredging up relics from the past son? The elevator opened and out from behind us walked Clara. Vincent stopped talking the moment he saw her, his playboy eyes gleamed. Clara however was stunned to see him. She approached us slowly. "Still beautiful." The old man smiled at her. "I have nothing to say to you." Clara said without hesitation, pushing the button to the first floor. "Understandable Ms. Jones. He followed us into our office. She leaned against the desk giving me the stink face. Believe me I was on Clara's side this time. "What the hell you want Vincent!" Vincent laughed rigorously. "I always did like you Clara, so feisty! I love feisty women. "Just not for your son, right!"she shot over at him, man that burn sizzled! He shook a finger at her. Now..now play nice. And let's leave the past in the past young lady. The Chief came in slowly staring at me surprised to see him too. I shrug my shoulders at him. "Vincent, can I help you?" He turned to the Chief. "Just came down to make a large donation to the Police Fund that's all. He unfold a check with a huge sum on it. The Chief didn't pick it up. "Thank you." he say instead watching the silver haired sly fox leave. He was in remarkable good health for a sixty seven year old man. "You all have a good day now." The elevators opened and out walked Mira. Vincent held his chest watching her walk towards my office. "It'll be illegal to lock up something so marvelous as you up."he laughed pushing the button to go down where all demons live. I was the first face she saw when she entered. Clara ..the next. She turned up the corners of her mouth.

"I got your message Miles you wanted to see me? Clara let out a small giggle staring at my relaxed trousers grinning. "Can you let us in on the joke Ms. Jones." Mira countered standing closer to me. "Oh its nothing." she said licking her lips at me. The Chief scratched his head, wondering what was going on now. Yeah Mira was a living doll when she dressed up and Clara the sex pot. "I wouldn't want you to get a rise so early in the morning."she whispered when she passed us. Her smile spread as generously as the bulge threatening to split my pants. Mira had quickly put two and two together. It wasn't hard to figure out Clara's little game. Mira pressed her body into mine running her heart shaped lips generously across them. The kiss was fire! And enough to knock the taste right out of Clara's mouth! "This ain't no social call Ms. Sylvester! Clara blew up, shoving her hand written evidence under Mira's nose! "We got you in the room with Camelo on camera! Are you gonna still stand there and deny your involvement in this, again? Yeah Clara was mad! "Mira stare up at me, I felt her tremble. "I am innocent Miles. "No over here Ms. Sylvester you're supposed to be talking to me! See I ain't no man! She said fanning her hands around the room. I don't fall for wide cow eyes, baby voices and tears!" That's enough Clara! The Chief demanded blocking Clara's way to Mira. "What?" You guys can't bring yourselves to arrest a beautiful woman?" The Chief was seeing bits and pieces of Clara he had never saw before. The woman has been friends with his wife for years. But something about this woman just brought out the worst in Clara! "Listen to me Clara." I said trying to keep a cool head. "Rufus had a damn good reason to kill Camelo. Rufus had a chance to go pro! But that dream was squashed by Camelo! What do you think that'll do to a man?" I got another angle for you Miles! Clara spit almost losing her voice yelling at me. Rufus is in love with Mira!"Tell me what that'll do to a man who wanted to protect her! Maybe go to jail!" She said out the blue catching me off guard. She must have caught something in my face telling her she had crossed the line! Because she did!

"Don't get it twisted, this is about the case Miles not us..she lied." I gently held her arm. I just came back from talking to Rufus, Clara." Uninterested!" she snapped pulling her arm away. "He knew about me and Mira, the same as you." I looked over at her... she smirked. "He called Mira dangerous. Wicked and born with a body to sin!" Why would he say those things about the woman he loved? "What you asking me for! I'm hormones not testosterone!" But if I didn't know better, I'd swear he was high Clara! I pressed on dismissing the remark." He sounds jealous to me!".. "Like you!" .."Why you!" Me and the Chief made it to Mira before Clara did! "Bring it bitch!" Mira was yelling! "Damn how many arms did Clara have!" Mira had sense enough to back away from those claws close to her face! I picked Clara up in the air and off her feet! And put her back down closer to the door! "I have a appointment Miles talk fast!"she spit with her eyes burning a hole in Mira! Clara words had come out hoarse." I could tell she was hurting. She could never hide her hurt well. The Chief turned forty one five months ago remember? I continued. We celebrated his birthday at the Sienna Club you and me. Well Rufus saw us there and so did Camelo! "Camelo even made a pass at you on your way out remember? She did remember. "Hey police lady, you here to arrest me?" he joked."..She ignored him while Carl poured her drink. I envy the man that climb that tree." He wolf whistled at her. That's why she left. "Get to the point Miles!" What I'm saying is, they both looked like jealous men, Rufus was dating Betty and Camelo was just a straight up player he was even hitting on her! But I sensed even then that Rufus had anger issues! Mira walked towards the open window, getting tired of Clara and all her accusations! Clara removed her earrings, this time, as a just in case. "Keep talking Miles your digging your grave!" The Chief laughed. If it wasn't for the seriousness of the case. He found their love comical!" Clara pulled out a cigarette, making a face at Miles. "You poor thing!"

"My point is Clara I have a feeling their both innocent! I'm just having trouble proving it right now!" Mira came up from behind me. "Its true me and Rufus was left in the room with Camelo alone Ms. Jones. I can't dispute that! I was holding my breath watching the two women energy play off each other. "Go on." Clara laughed. "Way to dig a hole for yourself, honey!" Ms. Jones I think you're a very smart woman and a brilliant detective. "Flattery now?" Mira waved Clara's attitude away. And both me and the Chief thought they had to be nuts! But Mira kept her cool. "What I'm trying to say Ms. Jones is, stop looking at the surface and dig deeper. Watch the tape the answer is there. I couldn't help but wonder if Mira was giving her a clue. "Fine!" Clara stumped more angrier then ever, getting all up in Mira's face. "Now let me tell you what half this town has told me about your woman here Miles. Rufus and her relationship went far beyond friendship!" That's a lie!" Mira insisted to her face! Clara took out a picture of them kissing tossing it to her feet. "I rest my case!" Sorry Miles." She left out the door, after giving me that hurtful look again. Mira turned to me and the Chief shattered. "And the next time you guys see two women fighting and decide to cape? Don't! Its a woman thing! She left us with that. But no explanation about the picture. "Is it me Chief because women have baffled me! "Don't think on it too much Miles, you'll hurt yourself. Its not for us men to know. The Chief left the office and I was back to square one!

 Clara was moving around in her kitchen finally washing her dishes later that evening, she couldn't sleep. We hadn't spoken for hours. "The boss told me they found earrings on the floor at the Sienna Club next to Camelo's body. According to one of the dancers Samara Green they belonged to Mira. The boss's wife Gloria helped her dry. "Why are you banging pots and pans around in your kitchen at this hour Clara?" she asked. Clara stood stock still staring around the room. "Tell me am I crazy Gloria? Do I want him so much I'd go to such petty lengths to hurt him? For somebody who wanted a open relationship, why am I so crazy why? We have so much history together. Gloria held Clara's hand saying. We go all the way back to College when we was roommates, Clara say to Gloria. "Come sit with me." They sit at the kitchen table. It smelled like Lemon Pledge like all of Clara's furniture. "You know Miles was very hurt when you decided to marry Wesley. He even left Hopeful and stayed away for years. Went back to that lovely home of his in Stunson. I was twenty two Gloria when I met Miles. You and I is twenty nine, now. Miles is thirty two now he and Wes are the same age. But Wes was so worldly! Wesley to my young eyes was everything! "I'm not here to judge you dear. But you forget you went off on a cruise with Miles right after Wesley made the announcement that he was marrying that

Socialite Payton Sylvester. Gloria's hand suddenly covered her lips. Oh I get now, she say in a hush tone of voice. "Payton, is Mira's sister right? Clara had long left the table to put away her crystal glass set Wesley gave her. She was staring into it. "Thing is Gloria, I realized how much I loved Miles on that trip. I thought of nobody but him the whole time. I was gonna tell him. I was so excited! Thing is when I got back to his house in Stunson, he was all cozy and wrapped up in a cover on his floor with some random! I saw them through the light curtains at his door window. "I was so hurt. Tears fell immediately from Clara's eyes that she could no longer hold back. "I'm so sorry Gloria I'm not use to being so weak. "Gloria hugged her smiling. "Don't be, its good to see my dear. A woman should be vulnerable sometimes. That's what separate us from the men. "Do you want him back Clara?" ..."Is it too late dear?" No answer, Clara just cried for the longest time. I couldn't sleep myself just kept pacing!

Chapter 7

Man I keep forgetting this was Clara fucking Jones! She was raised on a damn farm! Her family survived hardships by eating goats and calf's and potatoes for a living! But despite all of that Miss. Clara turned into a real fine young lady! So what did she see in my light skinned ass! Although taller than Mira by two inches she was still under me. Clara the stallion was definitely my type! She had drawn my eyes immediately when she stepped out her car for the first time! When I first laid eyes on her in front the police station eight years ago. Man I fell hard! But that was nine years ago technically and we been over! We was just used to each other. Found each other for sex every now and then like we do now! I heard a car screeched. She had doubled back? "Pay attention Miles!" She blast my ear drums off interrupting my thoughts! "Listen up!" Despite all that shit and bologna she fed you down at the station? I ain't buying it! I believe she Mira did it! And she's letting Rufus take the fall for it! So how do you like those apples Sherlock! Mira killed Camelo Miles! Why can't you see that! She slapped my face than kissed me soft on the lips, then slapped me again! Before running to her car! "Yeah she was hurt." I decided wiping my cheek. But sadly all I could think about even now..was Mira.

Mira took a slow ride back home in her Firebird to her mama's house. She shut the door behind her, reaching for her cell phone. Her moms house had originally been a saloon. However it made a better home. It belonged to Mr. Winston Kerr the son of the Tobacco Magnet, Mr. Colin Kerr long deceased. The son left the once thriving place fall in ruin. All that money his daddy invested in oil since 1930 with the Sweetwaters and he decided to open up of all things a saloon in Hopeful! Years passed and the roaches had long claimed the place. So he was more than happy to let her mama have it! The deal was if she could clean it she could have it! After that Winston went off got married and left town. They never heard from him again. But before leaving he gave her mama Sanita the keys. He even surprised the hell out of her offering a apology, for his rapist daddy! Sanita had worked for their family as a maid for years. Raised Mira and Payton in the backroom of the saloon on her meager earnings. His daddy was a penny pincher. Sanita tearfully excepted anything he could give her. And he always expected a piece of ass in return. It took years before Winston figured out that Payton was his half Negro sister. Unlike his daddy he didn't harbor any hard feelings towards them. So he was more than happy to leave the place to Sanita.

"Bout time you made it back girl!" Sanita grumbled shoving the swinging doors coming out the kitchen. "Where the hell you been? And where's my season salt! You lied and said you was going get my season salt Mira!" Mira yawned. "Don't tell me you forgot it again? "Mira!" She stumped irritated! Girl do I have to do everything myself?! Lord have mercy you'd lose your head if it wasn't attached to your body huh!" Thunder rolled Sanita shook her head closing the window. Mira rolled her eyes, falling back into the red velvet sofa, putting her feet up. "Geez moms can't you tell from all the make up I didn't go to no store." She started undoing buttons on her flowery Spring blouse fanning herself.

Miss. Mira Sylvester sat there on the sofa looking like a living doll."Well then answer my question then!" her mother was angry. "Well!" Mira helped herself to a nice piece of fried chicken. She had long ago gotten used to Hurricane Sanita! Besides the whole house smelled like fried chicken cooking. "Well you didn't need it, this taste fine. I went to church mama, there happy" she shrugged pulling off stockings. "Why you in a funk?" her mama asked reaching her a napkin. "Hard headed child, she finally say annoyed, answer me shit!" Mira's eyes fell on some letters on the coffee table in front her. "What's this?"

Her mama gave her a unreadable look. "Its your mail what else." Mom stop opening my mail. "Then stop having it forwarded to my house!" And I see you kept getting letters from Camelo, why? Mira raised a brow. "Where's the respect for the man mom he died almost a month ago." Sanaita sucked in breath. "I kept telling you he was no good Mira!' Oh you think you the only woman who's run into a sweet talker?" And how many times did I preached to your hot ass to stay out his club!".."I worked there!" Her mama sniffed suddenly smelled the gravy burning! Goodness gracious! And just like that she turned into a big floppy bird running into the kitchen! Mira got up following her in. They both fanned heavy smoke before opening up the kitchen window although it was still raining. "My life is my business mama so stay out it!" she stretched those wide cow eyes at her. "Here" . "They saying you killed him baby. Her mama say with her back to her. But there was no mistaking the pain in her voice. Mira took a deep breath. "That true Mira?" Mira handed her the towel instead leaving.

Sanita Sylvester was a widow now. And tough as nails. She went sit in her rocking chair lighting a pipe. The long stained dark green dress she wore almost everyday was full of flour from making chicken. She will wash it tomorrow. And the apron. Her long salt and pepper hair was in a bun. Sanita was still a pretty brown face short woman. She put on a hair net busing herself. Time had really taken a toll on the once beautiful fine forty eight year old. Sanita had given birth to twin daughters, sadly Mira's twin died. She had to depend on four mid wives to help deliver her babies. Soon after that her husband was drafted and had to go to war. He died over seas in active duty. Mira and Payton was all she had left now. The girls never knew their daddies and Sanita refused to marry again. Of course she could have easily had her pick of men in Hopeful, she was still good looking. Where do you think Mira's looks came from. She had a "friend" until he decided to marry since she had no intention to marry again. After that Sanita Sylvester preferred to be alone. Tears salted her still bright eyes this evening as she slowly crept back to the kitchen. The smoke had cleared. She stood in front her stove, then raised praying hands thanking god Payton married well. Her youngest daughter had married Wesley Sweetwater. She lived close by the lake and was going on baby number three. Everyday Sanita thanked God her younger daughter had made it out the ghetto. Yet somehow she always knew Mira would get stuck there. And end up in them mean streets! Dinner was ruined, so she got her umbrella and went to the store. She didn't mind eating cold cuts and a loaf of a bread tonight and Mira had to be fine with it too! Mira heard the door close, she sit up in her bed drying tears. She wanted to scream! Even her own mother thought she was a killer that hurt! Camelo was murdered at the Sienna Club! Ironically the place where he'd been so happy!

Chapter 8

The soft warm breeze was a welcome change in Hopeful later that evening when I packed my brief case. The sun even came back out. I wanted so much to go behind Mira when she left that elevator. I got outside too late, her car was pulling out the parking lot. I then decided to give her some time to rest and unwind besides I needed a shower myself. It was almost four o'clock straight up. When I took that long drive towards her house. It was times like this when I wish I could afford a better ride. Because my seven year old Ford Capri was slowly sliding to empty. My stomach growled noisily. Cause like a fool I hadn't ate all day. "Great" I said watching some kids running in the park playing b ball. Geez was I really that young once? I grinned. I had been so busy entranced in my work to actually enjoy the booming town of Hopeful. My lips went parched just remembering that wild night I spent with Mira. Could I really keep it just business today? Well I was about to find out. I turned the corner leading up Chickadee St. man who was in charge of naming these here streets! I passed close to Arnold's Seafood Shack just to get a whiff of all that seafood! When I got to Mira's place she answered the door in a white silk slip and nothing else. So much for keeping this just business."I had a feeling you would drop by Miles. "You missed me baby?" she moistened those lips slowly pulling me inside. I eagerly helped her out of that temptation hugging every inch of her curves! "Tell me you missed me Miles...no...show me." she was panting burying those long nails in my back. My wood caught fire! Mira was trouble and I was enjoying every bit of it! She moaned loudly against my ear barely breathing! You want me baby!" she licked the side of my face clean before wrestling with my tongue. Jesus she was on fire! Something wild juicy and soaking wet with cum sliding down her thighs! And she was all mine! "Fuck!" I lifted her slamming her against the door. My pants was biting into my meat I couldn't strip fast enough! I needed to fuck her! She didn't have to say a damn thing! Mira never did. What she wanted had always laid behind those sultry eyes. Our mouth devoured each others like hungry beast in that room! The bed almost broke! Nothing was off limits with her and nothing was like us! Mira was the other half of my damn soul! Something I couldn't explain to myself! Not even to Clara! I was invested in this case because of her. I was in love with her! So I had to do everything in my power to keep the Chief from locking her up for Camelo's murder! I let my mind traveled back.

(At the Sienna Club one month ago)

"Who's that?" Betty Cressy asked putting a cigarette between her lips. It didn't take long for the Palmer's Cigarette girls advertising box, to become lighter on their shoulders. So both headed back towards the bar for refills before more party goers came through the door. They stood closer to the gardens where Camelo had these intoxicating flower pots full of purple poppies going all the way up the steps of a interior designed New Orleans inspired balcony. Mira was drawing every heterosexual male eye in the house. Standing against heavy purple velvet drapes. That piano solo was a killer. The piano player Nathan Dalton played so softly his hands should be illegal in all fifty States! The tune filled the room with a sexual flavor a staple of course at the Sienna Club. Somehow or other I always figered that night I picked the pretty lady p in all that rain I wold see her again. "Mira..I said do you know him?" Betty squinted fanning smoke out her eyes before they passed near me. "No not really." she finally said refilling both their boxes. "He sure ain't from around these parts, from the looks of him. Girl he is too fine! Guys around here are more well fed then studs of that caliber, if you know what I mean! They both laughed." Betty was beautiful herself, I give her that. Her long sleek black dress came with three silver spaghetti straps that fell off the shoulders, plus she had a killer body. The up-swept hair do made her a beauty refined. They was both about the same height in heels and a tough call to make if all a guy wanted was to get laid. Betty giggled behind her hands. "Wow he's checking us out too look at him, god he's awfully good looking. I'll flip you for him Mira!" I appreciated the compliment coming from the beauty. They wasn't that far away from me not to hear everything. By the way Mira's eyes never left mine. Betty was a talker, Mira a observer. And of course I liked that a lot. Betty was smart too. It didn't take too long for her to picked pon the eye play between s "Oh I see where this is going she pinched Mira's arm playfully, well have fun!" Mira gave her a smile before she walked away. I was told the Sienna Club had very beautiful women up in there. They ain't neva lied! "You girls are doing fine, keep up the good work." Old man Vincent Sweetwater stops Betty pulling her into him fondling her in front of everyone very disrespectfully. Betty's good humor and smile was gone. "You liked that right darling?" He sipped his drank staring over at Marco giving him a nod.

Marco raised a finger in return paying Olson Palmer, the cigarette giant some money. "Ye..yess darling of course." her lips trembled. Betty knew exactly what he had mind when she saw Marco go upstairs with a maid. Mr. Sweetwater moved through the room with ease. The sixty something year old slime ball took Betty by the hand and led her upstairs. Mira frowned. Then I overheard people talking. Saying the rooms upstairs was for hook ups. And that Betty Cressy had been Vincent Sweetwater's later flavor of the month.

Just then a young woman in a stunning red outfit came sliding into the bar seat next to me clicking our wine glasses together. She was dripping in dubious fake diamonds but was oh so easy on the eyes. "Hello." she smiled big taking a sip from her glass. I nod, my foot slipped off the chair ,which drew a tiny laugh. "Carefl yo jst might be falling for me..she joked. I'm Lola Price the big busted woman brightly say, surrounded by all those bright lights looking like a red bone peacock ornament." Man her teeth was bigger and whiter than any I'd ever saw, peeping out of red lipstick! And that laugh sounded more like a sheep! Or perhaps the liquor was finally kicking my ass and I was being a total dick who knows! "Are you new here?" she actually asked through heavily pasted on eye lashes. She did that lagh again. Now if Clara was to come in right now, she would've had the woman arrested for imitating a sheep! "I was in a black tux and stiff white shirt, black tie basically a penguin sit! Like most of the fellas, well the outfit did called for the occasion. So who was I to talk about this woman. We was charmingly interrupted. "Uh huh" Mira cleared her throat. If you're interested sir. The mystery woman in the cream colored gown say to me over my shoulders. raising that satin gown two inches in the middle of her thighs, removing a card out a lacy cream colored garter belt. I'll be at the other end of the bar." I smiled taking the card and my drink with me. "Lola stood staring up at Mira impressed. "Well played."she smiled leaving. Mira nods as if they shared a commonalty only women was privy too. That soft piano was playing somewhere in the room in all that smoke haze. But it didn't matter, because if there was anything called romance left in this world it had showed up that night at the Sienna Club. Mira kept staring over at me as if trying to figure me out. That guy Marco seemed to be keeping his eyes on us as well, or maybe Mira. Making me wonder why. "Do you normally pick up men?" I asked as Carl the bartender filled her glass smiling at that. "Careful stranger he say to me Mira Sylvester's the freaky one in here!" They exchanged humorous glances as he wiped down the bar in front us. "Am not"...Mira pouted playfully. But something told me she was playing a game with me. A game of cat and mouse. And I think I was already chewing on that sweet cheese. "That's a loaded question." She stared down on me checking me up and down, removing earrings.

"By the way I'm Miles Prescott?" She stared at my offered hand before taking it. "Mira." Was all I got keeping me further in suspense. I cracked a smile at her, as those coy almond eyes swept me up and down one more time. Charmaine took center stage, and the whole place went quiet. She sung a very sultry song staring in our direction. Marco in all this time had come down and was standing by the piano immersed in the tune Nathan played accompanying Charmaine's lovely voice. They shared a smile. Carl was cleaning a shot glass staring in their direction. He then left the bar mad as hell and went out the back! "Do you trust me?" Mira asked quietly, bringing my attention back to her. Before quickly, getting up running towards the exit! I followed her of course. Outside we got inside her car. It was parked alongside a long wiry gate. She drove like a woman. Not too fast not to slow. Just like a woman. I wanted to laugh at my own nonsense. Then she floored it once we passed the red light! Afterwards Mira was nonstop! She drove so fast we scraped against a jigsaw turn pipe! She was driving the hell outta that poor sports car on a long stretch of road like a bat of hell! "To hell with traffic lights, I guess right!" I said trying to keep my cool. "I didn't kill him Detective." fell into the silence. That threw me off my guard. "You was the last person seen with Camelo. Do you want to tell me why?" Anything Ms. Sylvester. But all I got was more silence. Hopeful was a small sleepy town. Not much action. Except on the South side. Where the infamous Sienna Club stood. Mira had worked there prior to Camelo's death. "Where we going I asked after seeing a row of palm trees and nothing else! "Before I knew it, she pulled into a yellow marble pathway in front a huge estate. Was this her place? I wondered. "It was a decent enough structure. The long hallway was airy and spacious wide and breezy. Once you stepped inside that is. The living room alone could entertain about fifty guests easily. And the plush red rug under our feet was followed by another in shocking pink! I had been gazing around so long at the decor I had completely lost sight of the woman! "Hello Mira! I called. Where'd she go?" My detective instincts caught fire! The next thing I know I heard running water. It had to be coming from the bathroom. So I followed the dripping sound. Threw a crack in the door I saw her! "I hope you don't mind Miles." she splashed about in a gigantic tub. I just needed to freshen up a bit.""Will you reach me the soap behind you? My gaze never left the naked image. "Where?" She stood up pointing to it. "Your clothes detective, remove them." You always pick up men? I asked Mira again, with a sly smile, taking off my jacket. "No Miles...just you" My cell phone buzzed at that precise moment. It was the Chief.

Chapter 9

"What is it Mustard!" I cleared my throat saying staring at her. "Git your ass in gear Prescott! We got a murder on our hands remember!" And where are you anyways?" He asked bouncing a tiny infant in his arms. The baby puked all down his back from all that commotion! The baby's mama rolled her eyes and came got her tiny cupcake. "Clara's at the Sienna right now, looking for you. So where are you? I was in the bath tub by now getting sucked on in a very private spot. "Heaven" I told him. Talk to you tomorrow boss. I hung up. "Miles don't you dare hang up on me!..Prescott!..Hello? ..Damn it shit!" The Chief mumbled something I knew I would hear first thing in the morning! The next morning I sat up rubbing sleep out my eyes fighting a pounding hangover. My cell must have run a dozen times or more, well I was dreaming about cow bells, I did remember that! "I'm here boss what is it?" I hear my voice say. It sounded like it was coming out a long tunnel or something, but it still registered. "I'm surprised you're even home Casanova!" he bellowed with another lame snide remark hitting my sore brain! His first for the day. "Clara's sniffed out a new lead detective. She's already down at the Sienna Club questioning the suspect. And if we can prove she did it we're gonna lock her ass up too!" The sun rose right up in front of me, blinding my bloodshot eyes."Who is boss?" I asked knowing full well who. I was getting dressed more from memory then routine. "If Clara's there already its got to be about Mira." My heart sank.

Man my lover was trying to put my woman in jail! "Is it Mira? I asked anyway. I slipped on my gray tweed jacket checking my house phone calls. The Chief ducked the question. "Believe it or not Miles somebody saw four people that night leaving the scene of the crime not two. That's right, right around the same time as Camelo's death! We got a call stating two other women was seen running across the street in full blown traffic almost getting themselves killed! Right now the witness is refusing to come forward. Not surprising" he lifted his brows saying. "People in Hopeful do snitch!".. "Yeah I know" I agreed." Now I need you to find out Miles who made that accusation." The head honcho and owner of the Sienna Club was found lying face down in a pool of his own blood on the floor of his very own damn club! And was bleeding out when they found him. "You called Clara right Chief?" You should have spoken to me first you know, Clara hates Mira! "Well I tried!" he says exasperated. But you was dead to the world! "Mustard you know Mira isn't just another suspect to me." And I know you had a unit follow me and her last night, you slipping Chief! Mira floored her car and lost that tracker! She's not dumb! So you knew exactly where I was! Touche! Now that's the detective I know!" Clara's waiting and she's impatient. "I'm falling for her Mustard. Mira." Let me question her Chief. " I asked hopping around on one foot tying my shoe. He went silent. "I'll tell you this much Miles. Things ain't looking good for that woman." he hung up.

When I got to the Sienna Club, Mira was already being questioned by Clara! Man her face was so wet. I could tell she had been crying. Tears and mascara stained her pretty face. "Just tell the truth then!" Carla demanded in her lady detective voice completely ignoring me. Although she did saw when I came in. "I didn't do it!" Mira covered her eyes turning away from me. "Clara what are you doing?" I asked. All the color drained out her light brown face. "My damn job Miles!" What? She ain't getting no special treatment from me, just because she's sleeping with you!" Some laughter was heard around the room. "The Chief had entered in on Clara's latest burn and knew it was about me, from the expression on my face. "Let me question my girl then Clara." If nothing else she could tell when I was serious." For eight years Clara and I had worked side by side. And the amount of hurt I saw in her face right now, damn it wasn't worth it!" I should have told her I felt about Mira. "Oh really?" She said taken a back. "So she's your girl now?" Carla stretched the words staring around the room. "Well several of Camelo's employees in here just admitted that "your girl" was the last person leaving the back room she pointed, shortly after Camelo's death! "True or false Ms. Sylvester!"

Mira kept her eyes on me. "That's true detective, but I didn't kill him!" Mustard had arrived a few minutes after me. He leaned into Clara, remember the code detective don't badger the suspects. I think he was more worried about my reaction in all this then Clara's. "I did walked over slowly, finally taking her in my arms. Clara turned away. It felt wrong kissing Mira with Clara in the room. Mira however sanked into my shoulders feeling relieved. I kissed her again, I had to. She was trembling so bad! God I wanted to believe her! Carla tossed the handcuffs at me. "I'm outta here Chief." the Chief nods, understanding why. I was caught between two women that meant the world to me! And as I silently embraced Mira, I knew Clara needed me the most. Besides the police had caught Rufus going out the window."To me it was a done deal! Open and shut! I was being filled in on the case by one of the guys standing near the police chalk line. Al Camelo had been stabbed nine times in the chest it was a gruesome scene to say the least. I'm more than sure he knew he was dying before he hit the floor. The Hopeful Police Department had took him away in a body bag.

"They was lovers! I hear a woman scream hysterically from the back. She was breathing hard staring at me, with her make up running. I recognized her at once under those raccoon eyes it was Lola. "I caught you two myself!" she accused Mira. That's not true! Mira sniffed. Mira was scared and worried. From the look of her it was finally starting to sink in, she could go to jail! Lola was sobbing and grieving with the rest of the girls, they was all comforting each other. Mira had no one but me. And even Stevie Wonder could see Lola didn't like Mira! "You liar! She snapped at Mira. Who brought you that condo then! Camelo did!" And don't you dare deny it cause I could prove it!" Mira start to say something, then went silent wiping her eyes. The worst thing for me was, that the mumbling got louder in the room. "You screwed him the day before he died I walked in on you!" her voice thundered from somewhere deep down in her chest. "Get her statement!" The Chief yelled at me. But from the look on several of Camelo's employees faces, sadly Mira was being found guilty in the court of public opinion. Carla had been standing in the door listening to Lola. She heard everything. My mouth went dry for the first time in my life. Clara stared at me patting my shoulder. "You know..in all my years as a Detective Miles, she told me actually feeling sorry for me. It has always been a woman using a knife as a weapon! I told you this was a crime of passion, didn't I. Mira hung her head miserably staring at the floor. but kept repeating over at me. "I didn't do it." Call me stupid if you want too,but I believed her! The Chief had them pick up and arrest Rufus Lewis for the murder that same day. I was surprised to learn that not even the Chief was convinced Mira did it. Rufus was the one they caught after all going out the window with Camelo's blood on his hands! Clara looked at the both of us like we betrayed her! Staring at me walking out there with Mira. "You're wrong for that Miles!" she shout hotly! Beating the boss inside the squad car. I was convinced right then and there that these two women had history. What it was...I had no idea.

Chapter 10

Clara left the police station pretty late. She went back to my place first, finding me gone. Then stared down the hall way pulling a face walking away. At her house she tried to read a magazine but the tears kept falling out her eyes and rolling down her face. "Men are stupid!" she sniffed grabbing her coat running out locking the door behind her. Her head came up a hour later, She had fell asleep on the bar at the Sienna Club again. "Oh no how long was I out this time? " She asked Carl the Bartender. Him and Dolan the piano player pulled her up placing one of her arms around their shoulders walking her out. "Baby we don't count" Dolan smiled. "Thanks." Clara say sincerely. You guys are great! "Girl ain't no man worth all this! Dolan tell her, helping her inside his car. "I mean have you even met your fine self!" Clara laughed with Dolan and Carl actually felt better. "Tell me guys she asked Carl when they got to her place. "How you guys separate the job from the relationship? Dolan smiled staring lovingly at Carl when he got back in the front seat. "We just keep it real Clara. If you love this guy, Miles he said. She laughed. Then keep it real with him, tell him." Do you think Miles can do the same with you pretty lady?" He don't want me no more."She told them being honest with herself for once. Clara waved good night as they drove off. The guys said nothing to each other for a long time. "Miles is a fool." Dolan tells Carl obviously Dolan was team Clara. The one thing I've come to know about Mira if nothing else, is that although she was in a very disturbing situation, she lived her life without letting it break her spirit, well until now. "I missed you." she said to me out the blue, grabbing my hand as we walked that little ways to her house. We had to make a run for as the rain started coming down. Once inside, I gathered her dress up and planted kisses below her belly button before claiming the softness of her mouth. She pushed into me almost climbing me before shutting the door. To hell with any foreplay I buried my rod deep! She was already wet and I couldn't hide the bulge in my pants. I always rise so easily with her. The sex was the hottest I ever had with a woman with her panties still on! She bit my shoulders growling almost like a she beast as we curled into each other down there on the floor!

Mira heard my stomach growling then and bust out laughing! "Well now I'm starting to feel some kind of way detective! She purred like the sex kitten she is, putting a finger up bringing me into the kitchen. Tell me baby.."Is it food you want..then let me feed you?" I locked her arms behind her waist letting her fall slowly onto the kitchen table. "Ima greedy muthafucka! Can you feed me baby!" She breathed heavily into my ear as her female scent hit my nostrils removing those panties. I cleared the table with my hands hovering above. "Come eat." she stretched her legs wide spreading both sides of her pussy open with a index finger pulling it apart for me."I went under that yellow printed dress with my head. Determined to have all her mocha chocolate cake and eat it too. When we was together like this, the case and nothing else mattered! Afterwards we at Chinese take out in her bedroom. It was obvious Mira had gone somewhere cause she wasn't laying beside me anymore. "Hey" I say. "The Sweetwater's annual Spring Ball is in two days. "You want to go with?" She looked over at me smiling. "You mean with you?" Duh! I said enjoying her sparkling giggles. "If you want me to go, Miles sure." Good I said taking her closer. "You know Mira there's something about us." I said hoping she wouldn't laugh that off because I was being serious. "I know." she stroked the side of my face gently saying. "We fit." she sat up planting a kiss on my lips."Yeah" I agreed.

 I got dressed and once outside decided to call Clara. No answer, damn! I checked my watch. "Man it was that late!" It was imperative now more then ever that we wrapped this case! I put my hand on the handle of my car and two shots rang out putting bullet holes in my car and both my back head lights cracked out! I yank my piece out its holster looking around! Another one sounded really close this time! Somebody was trying to kill me! Mira ran out in a panic missing steps yelling my name! "Miles!" Two guys came running towards me in the darkness! Damn those trees made the perfect cover! It was so pitch black I couldn't see anything! And I think they counted on that! A shot hit the porch light this time near Mira, she froze! A police unit spin just a little distance ahead of mine screeching to a halt! They ran back tripping over each other jumping in their car speeding off! I couldn't see who was driving from the blaring headlights. The Chief got out and every nerve in my body started to relax. Mira had made it to me before he did. "Miles are you alright oh god!" she shivered in my arms holding me tight. "I'm fine baby." I assured her. But couldn't say the same for my jacket. The wind had blown my jacket out and in turn a bullet had torn through it. "I figured you was over here." The Chief nods at Mira even gave her a smile. "Thank god you came she breathed holding onto me even tighter. I am so grateful Chief. "Yeah Mustard I owe you." He pat my shoulders." Nonsense." Those was Cobra boys Miles. Damn now we got the Mexican gang Cobra involved? "Well Camelo was half Mexican remember, so my guest is they was after you Mira. "Mira's mouth fell opened. "Me!" Oh please believe me Chief I didn't kill Camelo!" The Chief surprised me. "I know." Mira looked stunned. He then went inside his coat pocket "Here, you go." I talked to that eye witness. He will get in contact with you too understand? "I nod my head taking the envelope from the Chief. Mira gave him a look I couldn't read. Was she covering up something? The Chief offered me a ride. "No Miles please stay!" her voice broke. I would die if something happened to you! So I promised I would.

The next day...

Clara stopped by the Chief's house to talk with Gloria. Their friendship went back years. "I meant to call you earlier Clara." she said bringing them tea. They both sit near a window. "Thank you." Carla smiled taking a long satisfying sip. "So how are you and Miles these days?' The gentle nurtured woman reluctantly asked. Carla stared at her peeping her eyes over the tea cup. "Me and who?".. "Oh I see." Gloria put in watching a very sad Clara staring out over her pool at the sun going down. "Don't be too hard on Miles my dear. "He's involved in a very trying case right now, well both of you are actually." Clara sat down her tea cup leaning back. "Oh he's involved alright Glo, with my number one suspect." Gloria shakes her head. "Are you really convinced Mira did it dear? Or is this really about Miles? You have to at least be honest with yourself if nobody else".. "I'm not ashamed to admit that its both! Her brows came together in a frown. "Oh dear." Gloria got up shoving her own cup aside. "Can I give you some advice then dear?" Carla smiled a bit. "Gloria we've known each other over nine years. Every since ol' Mustard hired me. she laughed a little."Gloria found that amusing too. Please stop calling my husband Mus-turd. "Nope, can't promise that. 'Okay. " They sipped tea laughing. "We're in our early thirties dear and not quite ready for a rocking chair yet . So why you giving your man to that little girl!" Oh believe me, she's a lot a lot woman she got Miles didn't she? The baby cried and they both laughed again. "You think the baby trying to tell me something Glo? I mean even the baby's even crying. Damn my situation gotta be very bleak huh? You are a beautiful and intelligent woman Clara. You'll find someone better trust me." "Is there better Glo? Yes my dear there is. And you're worth a man who knows what he have. Carla felt a little better. You think so? "Listen to me dear, honestly and all bullshit aside? I have come to know both you and Miles pretty well. And I have a feeling this thing between him and this woman Mira ain't nothing but a fling, you'll see!" Clara brightened up. She went around and hugged Gloria. "He loves you sweetie pie, I could see it." Gloria walked Carla to to the door. "Good night Glo." she leaned in kissing her on the cheek, feeling very much relieved. "Drive carefully now!"she waved as Carla ran to her car. "I will bye."

Chapter 11

In the days that followed, I was expected to turn in my final report. I have learned so much about this case. I stood in my window watching a migration of black birds flying south. I begin recapping everything told to me, standing there closing my eyes. Man the things you learn about people living in a small town. Later that night Charmaine Lewis was the dark beauty right now pulling out all my fantasies and deepest recollections of when I first met Clara. Charmaine was singing that song Just You. "Just You" was our song, mines and Clara's. Clara was seated in the back of the Sienna, and she wasn't alone. I pretended not to notice when see arrived with Wes Sweetwater. They was both impeccably dressed. But she looked absolutely amazing! Stunning..really! We shared a reminiscent glare over at each other. It was nice of the Chief to have them reopened the club. Otherwise over sixty people would have been unemployed. Everything seemed back to normal. Charmaine's eyes fell into mine when I turned back around. She was moving closer to our table where I was seated hand in hand with Mira. I sat there confused. She was singing that song why? Mira seemed furious.

She sanged. "There was passion in his grip! And love all over his lips..I was tripping you was slipping..But no matter what we do..You was mine..candle to flame..not alike..but still the same..And all through these blues..Tell me baby..Tell me the truth...When love came around even after good byes..Why would it always look like just you...You knew how to please me..You even teased me..There could be no other ..no better lover..With you can't you tell..I'm under a spell.. And oh how much I want you. Cause your love rock my world..my toes even curl.. And I just can't stop loving you..Tell me baby..When love come around.. without sight or a sound..why it always look like...just you. That was the night Coffee had come through the doors in a penguin suit, and seated himself in the front. Staring at Charmaine. I think he was trying to impress her. He cleaned up pretty good too bad he wasn't good! Charmaine took notice of him anyway, even slightly smiled. Five days earlier, she hesitated opening the door to the Sienna Club. Some of the old crew was in there cleaning the place. She waved at several of them. It felt so errie being back there. Thoughts of her and Camelo came flooding back like a bad movie scene. The floors of the Sienna Club was all dingy now. Not the brightly polished shine so clear you could see your face in it that was gone! Then there was the long yellow police tape around the crime scene still in front the back door. She didn't have the stomach to venture any further to the back. Girls had been hanging with the fellas that night partying and drinking! It was Saturday night and the drinks had been flowing at the Sienna Club since happy hour started at 12 o'clock! The popular club was indeed living up to its sordid reputation!

Al Camelo stood over some guys dealing cards all wrong, with smoke choking his lungs. Yeah he was that close to their cheating asses. She was up next. His main attraction! He set nothing and no one above her when it came to that stage and spotlight! She at least had that. She stood there closing her eyes hugging herself. Not even his popular dancers, which included Mira could top her. Charmaine's vocals was now the talk of the town because of him! And she looked very beautiful and sultry in that white satiny velvet sequinced gown he brought the twenty five year old after banging her that evening. The dim lights bounced off the floors in rainbow colored lights circling her sleek frame to perfection. She was called the Siren of Wet Dreams and The Queen of the Sienna Club! Camelo had given Charmaine that name. Charmaine sniffed moving just a bit further into the room. She remembered his funeral. Al had been laid out in a chrome green platinum casket. He wore a green suit and tie a pristine white shirt and his hair had a fresh wave. Everything was mostly green even most of the flowers had to have some green in it. The color green was his favorite color. The color of money. His mother Carlotta Camelo held the hand of her only surviving son her oldest son Luis. The woman looked frail as she blew her nose leaving church. Her daughters Magdalena and Marie had to catch a flight there, so they was late. But their mama was so happy to see them arrive.

Charmaine was the only black person allowed to be seated with the family and at the grave site. Al's mother Carlotta and aunt Anita and the rest of the family knew how much Al loved Charmaine. He had brought a ring. And planned to ask her to marry him the next day. A ring she never wore. Despite the fact that Al Camelo's father was a high yella Negro with some Spanish running in his veins. The rest of the Camelo family she found to be very traditionally Mexican. Charmaine was the only one excepted into the fold. Al had been cheesing really hard from ear to ear staring around at all his satisfied customers. Whenever Charmaine took to the floor in any unmistakable sequined ball gown paired with that beautiful voice. All he could smell was a over flow of money! Camelo was rich now, a millionaire. The girl was his wet dream and gold mine all in one! Over to the left his eyes caught sight of Mira Sylvester crossing the floor, in a long black shimmery clingy number. She was his naughty dream. Mira wore her long black hair bone straight tonight and pinned to one side with a jade barrette, giving off some quiet elegance in the smokey club. The green heels matched the barrette she was totally the face of romance. Al removed his cigar slowly from his mouth, just gawking at her in a trance. His dark brown suit almost collected the spittle falling out his mouth. He messed his dark brown hair up trying to compose himself.

She was also one of many cigarette girls hired that night by Palmer's. Why on earth would something like that be passing out cigarettes at a club made no sense! He thought it a crime! Al considered making Mira a good investment and her good looks a plus! He couldn't help but notice how men crawled all over themselves to get a pack of cigarettes from her. The shapely sun kissed twenty five year old short stature beauty, kept her cool, instead of driving off his costumers. He liked that. He planned right there to hire Mira and put her on the pay roll. "Sir?".."What!" Camelo growled. The bartender Carl interrupted his scheming plans slipping a note in his hand. He stared down at it frustrated before crumbling it up! "Look he squeezed Carl's shoulder roughly. "You go on back over there and tell that rotting teeth Coffee he'll git his damn money when I say so! Now leave me the hell alone Carl! Shit nigga can't you see I'm busy!" he grumbled shoving him out his way. "Sure thing boss." Carl cut his eyes at him pissed as fuck following them over to Mira. Camelo then made his way over to her without taking his eyes off her.""Well well well...look a what the cat dragged in." he chuckled offering her a drink. "Meow" Mira smiled. He blew smoke on her. Charmaine sniffed coming out that foggy place in her brain. "Why Al?"She lifted a bottle off the shelf from behind the bar popping the cork in tears. "Why out of all the girls in the Sienna Club. You just couldn't stay your ass away from Mira." She jumped almost out of her skin when she heard the door open again! Charmaine blinked wildly. "What are you doing here Coffee?" He said nothing, just opened her hand and placed the item in it. "I think this belongs to you." It was Camelo's father's watch. "Charmaine closed her eyes holding against her stomach. "Thank you." she whispered. "No problem Charmaine. " he told her sincerely, turning by the door, before stepping out back into the sunshine.

Chapter 12

"Oh good Miles you still up." Clara said clicking off the lights. My dizzy head came up out the cloud of my own typewriter as she stood in my doorway. My eyes was blood shot. And without even knowing it, I had pulled another all niter. I had on my black robe over my white under shirt and black boxer shorts. I must have dressed in my sleep. "Its all a part of the job my lovely you already know that." I informed her irritated. And I bet you haven't slept a wink!" She shook her head at me, watching me wipe my eyes. "Your such a child sometimes." I rested my head on her belly. "Yes I am." Clara tilted that chin of hers sucking in air. She looked like a black Betty Boop caricature period! With a page boy hair cut and bangs to boot! And her style was definitely refined and classy. She wore fox furs everyday the real ones nothing fake! She wore those fox tales with everything! She dressed in long flowing satin dresses that was really pretty. Her favorite colors was soft yellow, soft pinks, soft reds and beautiful earth tones. I only see her in black and white on special occasions. And with every outfit the woman wore a hat! This morning she was wearing a small white bowler, with a dark blue pin stripe suit and a long light blue fox tail around her neck. Oh well so much for me making sense out of of women's fashions.

"Clara what time is it?' I stretched before yawning. She stood me up turning me towards the clock. "Its eight o'clock in the morning Sherlock." Miles I'm starting to worry about you. Clara went put on a pot of fresh coffee. "Well don't." I frowned walking around in my bare feet. All this happened the day she drove up to pick me up from Mira's mother's house. My car had a hole in it and the tail lights was gone. And Cobra's thugs also managed to hit my gas tank! Mira was frightened for me and begged me to spend the night. She was at her mama house. Mira's mother's house smelled like burnt smoke. But Mira insisted I stay. We went hot and heavy in the sheets until the crack of dawn. Mira's mother Salita was bringing Mira breakfast on a tray yesterday morning. When she saw me leaving Mira's room. "Oh my." she gasped with her hands to her chest almost dropping it. "I nod at the lady fixing my clothes before leaving her house. "Mira giggled at her mothers expression. Her mama didn't find it funny. "I reminded the woman detective my lover and partner in crime, how stubborn she could be herself when it came to solving cases. "Besides you know the drill" I said. This our final report my love and its due on the Boss's desk tomorrow. Or that giant turd Mustard will be all up our asses with a Pogo stick! She made a face trying to look like him. Why do you get all humorous Clara when I'm tired? She beamed flipping her hair at me laughing. I hugged Clara. She hugged me back. I had actually missed my partner yesterday. Being locked away from the world like that! Imagine being best friends with such a woman for nine years. She worked my shoulders until I almost fell asleep. "Mustard would dock our pay if you didn't turn in something, she reminded me. The cynical fool!".. "Hey he just turned forty and had a baby. We should cut him some slack, don't you think?" I yawned big." She picked me up off the sofa leading me to my bedroom. "I'm putting you to bed right now!"

 "Promise?' I jokingly said bending leaning on her shoulder. Inside the room she begin removing her clothes before I took off any of mine! Clara had stripped down to a tiny silky white slip and lacy white drawls catching me off guard. I got that morning wood so fast, and didn't know what to do with it! "Besides Miles you do know I'm jealous." She was back in my arms. "Say what?" I asked puzzled. "Oh I wouldn't call her a what dear. No, she's more of a who. I kissed the lips of the woman I had been bedding for nine years. I knew what she was hinting at. Or should I say ...who. "Mira is down at the police station right now, along with the other suspects." she tells me. Biting on my bottom lip. "Why is she there Clara?" Obviously just like a man your clueless?" But it was obvious Clara wasn't." Why Clara?" She sat up in bed, looking more serious than I'd ever seen her. "I don't mind our open relationship Miles. But if you're trying to make me jealous, you've won okay? "And to answer your question. Its because we got just as much evidence proving Mira is just as guilty as Rufus." She stroked my chest curling that light brown cashmere smelling body into mine. "I mean sure I've dated Wes Sweetwater for a minute. But I still let you hit. Damn right, I said slipping down those panties. "Ooh this is fun! she squealed as I tasted that belly button."I'm going to the Sweetwaters Ball tomorrow night. Maybe I'll get a chance to talk to Mira about the case.".. "I prefer you not." Clara covered my lips with her own.

Chapter 13

The noise from the coo coo clock on the living room wall made Charmaine more stressful then she already was! She went shut it off. Camelo had gave her that clock. Why couldn't she stop thinking about him even now! "So why you here." Camelo's hand had cupped her knee, she removed it...Charmaine sat there pissed as a greedy ass Camelo counted his money. "Why you bring Mira home last night?" he smiled. "I didn't she hitched a ride." He then poured them both a drink. "Remind me to fire Carl ass will ya" his eyes traveled over to his bartender. He then reached over to hug her this time, but she pushed him away again! "Don't play me for a fool Al! I ain't one of your naive hoes out here!" She hollered that part louder than he was comfortable with. "Baby look I told you" he shifted his position lowering his eyebrows as well as his voice, watching his guest paying too much attention to them instead of minding their own business! "Listen its just you and me sugar I told you that! Why can't you believe me honey? And besides baby doll Mira's your friend not mine! he shurged. I met her through you, remember my lolipop? And its because of you, I'm friendly with the chick. I love you girl just you! Char I want only you! And I could prove it. He reached inside the pocket of his black suit just before Coffee kicked him out his seat dragging him outside!" "Let's talk Hombre." Coffee twisted his arms breathing in his face!

 Charmaine pulled herself out of bed. How long was she gonna hear his voice. She wore nothing ..staring out at the sun. She then went into the bathroom to pee on a stick again praying it was wrong. But discovered she was already wet between the legs. She also wondered how long it would be until she stopped having wet dreams about him. Charmaine washed her face staring at herself in the mirror, three months pregnant. The door bell buzzed so she grabbed a robe and went opened it. "Hi." a energetic Camey waved.."Camey?" she said in bewilderment walking out grabbing her robe. Camay followed her around, staring at her messy apartment. "Instead of calling you I decided to pop in! Can you guess what day it is Char go on?" She urged stretching her wide slanted eyes hopping up and down sounding five! Charmaine busied herself by slipping into the pink mini dress and panties Camelo gave her on their Bermuda trip. Camay was such a Christian. She covered her eyes, then went back in her closet and dug out another pink dress. It was more longer and conservative falling pass the knees." And here." I like this red button jacket, it goes well with the dress. Charmaine got goose bumps putting it on. She remembered that outfit only too well. It was the one she wore the day she met Camelo! "Why would you give me this outfit instead of something else!" she barked at her sister looking hurt. "Still she couldn't help but stare at herself in the mirror. "Camey I met Al in this." I'm sorry I didn't know.

 "Al was in the parking lot of the church. And I walked pass him. He instead ran behind me and I broke out in a cold sweat!" She said smiling. "Girl ..no man had ever affected me like that!" Al was short but he was cute! And his body was fit as hell!. Camay squished her eyes together. "Oh right, sorry Ms. Christian." she joked. I mean, he had a decent build to himself. Camelo didn't work out much but you could still see he had muscle tone. His light colored skin and eyes spoke to his heritage. He was half Mexican and half black and I was full black and he admired that!" He was a self made man, Camey."Camay dropped her eyes away staring around the room instead. She didn't want to say the wrong thing. "Did you know Al used to sell jewelry for a living him and his brother Marco?" No that's right,you was too young to remember that. They worked at Penny's Jeweler Store over on Selena's. Ever since he was in high school, Marco use to cut diamonds. He let Al sold gold chains. Marco was arrogant and don't like girls! Still you'd be hard pressed to find a single person that didn't know Marco and Al Camelo here in Hopeful."

"Al became the owner of the infamous Sienna Club. A club with a horrible reputation. The club wasn't called that back then Camay. It was known as The Blues Club." Once owned by a black gangster by the name of Jeffery Muntz. Muntz shot the man who ran the place back in the late 1900's killing him. After he found him looting his meager pennies out his safe, that he kept stashed in his barn yard behind a haystack. The money Muntz put away was enough to buy the place off the rich white investors who owned the Blues Club. He hid a cool thousand dollars in there. That was money back then. Muntz took over the place. He believed it was a gold mine and he was right! Back then it was considered strange to see black owners of night clubs in small towns. But since it was a colored club and white folks lived clear across on the other side of the tracks separated by a long stretch of woods. The colored resident felt free to enjoy their only place of entertainment. Of course The Sienna Club looked nothing like it does today. Back then it was no larger then a small living room and a bedroom put together. It had a bar, some stools, a beer barrel, some tables and chairs and a guy playing piano in the corner.

And a bunch of Jazz bands would play at the club, on a Saturday night! The club soon became a fixture in the 1950's, after word got out that Muntz paid good money for entertainers. And subsequently the tiny club's reputation grew more and more. It later expanded and started filling the place with dancing girls like the other clubs. The Sienna Club became a hot spot for affluent black people like us after that. People use to hang outside having fun! Indeed the club flourished beautifully! And the well to do black folks soon edged out all, the poor black people. They built a tall brick wall in front the entrance of the door. Where two body guards stood protecting it. The guys was salty at first, but then started tossing dice at the wall. The betting started and the wall became so popular even the rich folks and the body guards joined in on the fun!. The club got really successful once rich folks of all races started filling it, in the 1970's. At the age of eighty one years old Jeffery Muntz died. And in his will he left the club to his oldest son Wilson Muntz. Wilson was sixty, but had a young wife Sabina. She gave birth to a baby boy at the age of forty one. Their child was named Carl Muntz. Soon after that, bad luck befell Wilson Muntz. His wife Sabina was killed in the terrible flood in 1996. Wilson was too much of a business man to raise his own son. So he put Carl up for adoption.

And wouldn't you know it. The Sienna Club would end up eventually in the hands of The Sweetwaters. Camay made a face. The Sweetwaters was too busy mining their oil and gold mines. But considered the club a good investment. They are the wealthiest black family here. So it was easy for the Sweetwater's to put money into a establishment called the Sienna Club since it was already booming. They put the club on the map! And gave it all the prestige its famous for today and around the world. The club was brought with smuggling money Camay, and ran on gambling debts. Wilson Muntz had a partner, Rick Rice. He caught him stealing their profits! Muntz never really trusted him in the first place. Because Rick was underhanded enough, to try and sell Muntz property right back to some rich white folks! Just so's he could buy it back and run the Sienna Club himself. Now Muntz's friend Cletus Ross had two beautiful daughters. And Wilson Muntz started dating his youngest daughter Norma Ross. To keep Rick's hot hands off the place. Camay stared spellbound. She was actually astounded and impressed that her sister had taken the time to learn the origins of the Sienna Club. It must be high noon, she was thinking. Judging by the sunlight on her dark shades and the time on her wrist. Cleatus sold his connecting property to Muntz, Charmaine continued busying herself folding her clothes back and sticking them up in the closet. The men struck a deal. It was agreed that Muntz would marry his daughter Norma who loved Muntz anyways. Her father asked but one thing. That Muntz dropped the name The Blues Club and renamed the place Sienna in honor of his wife. Sienna Ross had perished from a high fever. With Muntz owning the connecting property now, The Sienna Club was finally secured from all investors!

The place then became known as The Sienna Club after that day. And soon afterwards, about a year or so into the marriage, Muntz lovely wife Norma was found dead in their bed from fixation. Somebody had smothered her in her sleep. Obviously to get back at Muntz, for that thief Rick. After a respectable grief period, Wilson Muntz remarried thirty three year old Sara Sweetwater at the age of sixty three. Giving her the deed to the Sienna Club as a wedding present. He had married into Hopeful's richest black family and didn't know it. He died before the family discovered all that oil. Sara later remarried Jose Camelo and gave birth to their only child, Marco. "Okay I get it now, Camay said taking a seat. That's why the Sweetwaters hired Marco, he was family. And then Al's mama married Jose after he divorce Sara Sweetwater for cheating on him. And Al's mama Carlotta gave birth to two sons and two daughters. Camelo being the youngest son. And because of the Sweetwaters connection the Sienna

Club got even richer. The Sweetwater's owned just about everything in Hopeful. And just about everything had their name on it. Especially a lot of the property. Even the church grounds, the cemetery and the Senior Home not to mention Starlight Adoption Agency. In his will Wilson Muntz put a clause. Although Carl went to a nice family in Hopeful.

He asked that the Sweetwaters would keep him employed. Vincent hired him as Sienna's Bartender. Wesley Sweetwater their oldest and now thirty nine is a doctor running his own clinic. He and Marco is close friends. Has been like forever. Wesley didn't want to run the club. And Marco being Vincent and Wesley's hired man when it came to their business affairs. Felt the club would never make him a millionaire. So he gave it Al Camelo's brother Luis Camelo. Two years later Luis got an emergency call from his family in San Juan he was needed. Their father had passed away. Luis was now expected to run the family's restaurant business which happened to be Luis's dream job. The family counted on Luiz to make sure they didn't get stiffed anymore by any of those fast talking Lawyers his father hired. And seeing no one else was capable of running The Sienna Club, Luis it to Al. For Luis, Al was the only logical choice. He didn't trust their half brother Marco in the least. Simply because he was a Sweetwater. She took a breath. Marco had been a drug addict. Booze cocaine you name it he done it. Even living off women when he wasn't in the streets! He owed his life to the Sweetwaters. Because they cleaned him up and gave him a job. He became their gopher. And he seemed to enjoy his job. Marco was handsome then and he still is. But he couldn't hold a candle to Al's good looks. Camey yawned, she was just glad her sister had finally finished the history lesson.

Chapter 13

Charmaine went silent. Camay saw a tear drop out her eyes. "Hey you okay?" Charmaine heard those words from somewhere, as if they came out a long tunnel. Her mind was drifting again. "I'm Charmaine Lewis she giggled,delightfully. Al stood there taking her hand. "Wow you're very beautiful." he said. A real life Barbie doll! We both laughed. She remembered, that she was indeed in that nice church outfit Camay found. Who knew Camelo would be her destiny. Al had to admit that Charmaine was fine as hell! She had that going for her also. Beautiful dark glistening skin, the girl was easy on the eyes. A richness she was to him flawless. Al was in love. Big sexy brown eyes, a bright sparking smile and shoulder length long black wavy natural hair that hung on top of her shoulders. Charmaine Lewis to him was wifey material. But was he even ready for a wifey? He was sure he wasn't worthy of this Nubian Queen! The wheels was spinning off the spokes even back then with Camelo. Al Camelo forever the business man! "I promise Charmaine believe me baby all I want is you!" "She heard his voice say out loud. Or was it inside her head. Her eyes finally focused on her sister. God was she going crazy! Talk about a snake in the grass! She was frowning now. She just couldn't stop thinking about him! No better he was slime! Camey stood up worriedly. "Are you alright sis?" Charmaine found out too late that lying came so easy to Camelo! Her anger was kindled so much and so was her wrath! It was all over her face! I understood that type of anger. It was righteous anger. "The scum!" she screamed pacing the floor. He had left Charmaine sitting at the bar. And was being carted off by Coffee and his low life thugs! And when he did emerge again from the back room. He came out with a busted lip! She was in no mood for his sob story! But deep down she kept smelling a rat! And it was wearing Old Spice cologne a white suit and black tie! Al had hurt Charmaine deeply!

"Hello? ...hey girl are you still in there? Where'd you go!" Camay knocked her on the head softly staring dumbfounded. "Look sis, she says nervously sitting her down in a chair, holding her car keys. "Lets just go and get outta here for a bit okay? We can just take a drive anywhere you want. I mean its just feels so eerie up in here right now Charmaine! she shuddered. I mean its like you could just feel Camelo's ghost hanging around here or something, she wined. Girl its fucked up creepy alright!

Charmaine pushed her aside running towards the stairs pulling at her long unruly hair screaming like a mad woman! "I'm pregnant Camay! Now just get out of here okay! Just go the fuck home before you worry mama! I don't want to see you or anybody today! I can't handle this right now oh god! she kneel at the bottom of the stairs with her eyes darting left and right. Camay started crying. ""Sis WHY! Why do you have to defend him huh? she choked on her own tears wiping her nose. Charmaine! He wasn't even good to you! Camay shot bitterly to her face, watching Charmaine's hands tremble lighting a cigarette. Girl don't do this to yourself, you pregnant! Char! she sniffed rubbing her sister's back. Al was a low life! Lower then scum okay a man whore! She hollered louder than she intended too. "That's enough bitch! Charmaine grind her teeth coldly. Look just go! She rocked her legs nervously. I said get the fuck out here! She grabbed her sister's shoulders shoving her to the floor! Its my birthday Char! Its my birthday! Camay shout shaking her head miserably.

 How can you treat me like this! Charmaine went down next to her sister tossing away the bud, before scooping her sister in her arms. Oh baby girl I forgot. Oh god Kay Kay I am so sorry. Camay was nineteen now but was still being treated like a child in the family. She hated it! "You have no idea what its like to be a woman Camay! Charmaine sobbed. She stood back up holding her stomach staring down at it! I do know what its like to be a got damn woman damn it cause I am one! Charmaine wiped Camay face. "Of course you are."the words meant nothing to Camay. I want to go to the Sweetwaters anual Spring Ball. Its in two days. Will you go with me Char? Charmaine smoothed back her hair. Do you guys have paternity wear down at the boutique? Camay smiled gathering her things. "Please forgive me Camay, I'm just not feeling well. I guess its all these hormonal changes, please understand. Charmaine kissed her on the top of her like a child. "I'll see what I can do." Camay breathed deeply heading towards the door. "Camay wait! I do have something for you!" She ran up stairs and came back down excitedly with the necklace she had brought for her last week. "Ta da!" she looked around for Camay she was gone. Charmaine ran outside a little ways after her sister's car. Camay stared at her in her rear view mirror but kept driving. Charmaine held the necklace against her heart sadly. "Camay." she said before going back inside.

Camelo was laying between broken crates I was told. Before receiving those punches from Coffee. I tell her" I sucked on one of Clara's perky raspberry nipples then the other. "Who told you that?" She moaned with her hands squeezing my dick. Making it rock hard! "Wait let me guess she propped herself up. " The bartender Carl Bower he had Coffee beat him up didn't he, am I right?" I lower my face to her private part stroking it deliciously with my tongue ..she gasped biting her index finger. "You got it baby they had bad blood between them." I said, managing to mount her easily taking my seat above her hairless throne. "Mummmm ..yesss..oh Miles yessss only you can do me so good. She was moving in that circular motion I liked making me forget about sleep! Her pussy was wetter than a leaky faucet! Which meant Wes wasn't hitting it right! Besides the day was young and I wanted all of her!"That nice white suit Camelo was wearing somehow miraculously stayed looking permanent pressed didn't it babe!" She managed albeit with some difficulty swallowing my per-cum. since I backed that thing up against the bed! Clara turned around and locked her legs around my hips and I almost lost it! "The black tie Camelo had on was choking his neck..she squirted! I must have hit that G spot! And before long we both felt the on rush of our climax. It poured on us like rain! She sat up fixing her hair back. Then gave me a long satisfied kiss. Clara left my bed and went picked her slip off the floor. "Miles talk to me." I lay there sliding my hand down the length of her long legs. "Is we fooling ourselves here? And yes, I'm talking about you and me now?" Clara just had to kill the mood. "You want the truth baby?" I said. .."I can handle the truth yes please." she said sitting next to me. " I'm more than attracted to Mira Sylvester, Carla." After that Clara seemed different. She left and I went back to reading my report.

"I told you Coffee ...Camelo spit blood!. I'm going to contact Reed Sampson for you he got real good connections! But if you keep being a dick about it and can't wait! I ain't giving you shit! He surprisingly fought off both Coffee goons pretty good a onlooker told me! Before they plummeted him in the side! But anger has always did and always will give a man extra strength! Coffee grunted something about taking Charmaine away from him! And Camelo lost it! I told you to keep your grimy hands off what's mine! Camelo was having trouble breathing after the pounding Camelo gave him! "Call off your goons off nigga call'em off!" Camelo spat. His hounds was shocked that a man no taller then 5 feet 8, could take down a man 6 feet 2! His goons started pounding on Camelo mercilessly again, trying to kill him! "Oh shit!" One of the men yelled, after spotting four big stocky corn bread fed fellas running towards them! They was being thrown around like feathers in the alley! And all them had their face smashed ignore a broken nose! Coffee fell onto a car staring at his men receive the beating of their life! Nobody expected that Camelo had friends! Al's muscle had indeed arrived! Al wiped blood from his mouth. He was gonna need stitches but didn't care. Coffee's goons then took off leaving their boss Coffee for dead! That's enough!" Camelo tell the guys pulling Coffee off his expensive car, and putting him against a wall. Camelo's lip was slit pretty good and it was swelling. He could barely feel it! "Okay you piece of shit! Now its my turn! Camelo's heart almost sank after Coffee held up his daddy's heirloom gold watch laughing. The gold piece had always dangled off his vest. It was the last gift his daddy gave him. "Come on man." Camelo pleaded with Coffee, sticking his hand out. Okay alright! I'll get you your money today fuck! "Good, then I'll hang onto this until you do nigga." Coffee spat blood slowly sliding his bruised body to his house.

Chapter 14

 We was nearing the end of a very difficult case. I had to take out time to process it all! Cause stuff like this will surely drive a man crazy! Dealing with this bullshit on a regular basis and at the same time having my personal life falling apart, was beginning to take its toll! But this is the job I signed up for and one I was pretty good at it! So I really shouldn't complain, should I? Because at least the people here was quick to supply me with all the information I needed. Or otherwise I would have a ton of shit to dig up. I thought about Clara flipping through the pages. I missed her.

Charmaine was having trouble herself processing her own present situation. She stood in the middle of the floor staring up at the stage that felt like a second home to her. Replaying back in her mind her life with Camelo at the Sienna Club. "Why did you have to have her..nigga" Why Mira? She took a seat trying to make sense of it all. Maybe Lola was lying! She wanted to believe Lola had lied to her! As painful as it was and as hurtful as it was to forget what she told her, she couldn't stop remembering seeing Mira run in the club that day dripping wet, drawing all the men eyes! In that moment she had felt so much rage! And all the good times they'd spent together growing up and up until now had simply vanished! In that moment she had really hated her best friend!

Mira ran into Charmaine just as Charmaine was leaving the club. Unaware that this was a Charmaine who was even more pissed then before she came in! Mira had paid the taxi fare on the way in, before rushing into the Sienna Club removing her rain cap and umbrella shaking rain drops out of rain dampened hair, drawing the eyes of every man there. Charmaine stared around furiously, if Camelo would have came out and saw Mira she would have lost it! Mira was wearing a black V neck halter top today with some tight fitting blue jeans. It was more closer to Summer now then to Spring. Her long hair hung down her back wind blown and dripping on the ends. Large gold hoop ear rings dangled from her ears disappearing into all that hair. Even the weather couldn't destroy her stunning good looks! It had been pouring rain since that afternoon. So what else was new in this shanty town that seemed to always be crying? Charmaine snapped! She surprisingly hauled off and slapped Mira in the face so hard for all it was worth! I can't stand you!" she steamed with so much venom. "And stay away from my man you fuking whore!" Yeah right, this is what she shouted at her best friend for life, before knocking her out her way rushing out! Mira's face stung from the pain but more from what came out Charmaine's mouth! Embarrassment washed over her as she stared around at all the people looking on in disbelief. Camelo had seen it all! He'd come out the back room just in time staring at the two women just as stunned as everybody else. "Come here." he called to Mira to follow him. Al gave Mira a ice pack for her swelling cheek after they got to the back. "Thank you" she sniffed refusing to look at him. "What just happened Al!" she finally let the hot tears run down. Al hugged her. "Damn it baby, I don't know why Charmaine act like that sometimes! "Listen..cut her some slack okay? Damn, he said watching the black and blue knot puffing out her jaw. She should at least apologize you know. He massaged her back, slowly letting his hands undo her halter top. Al thought he was being slick. Mira's eyes stretched. "What the fuck you doing?".. he chuckled a little "Oh come on don't act so surprised now! You know you want this!" She push him off "You crazy! Her right cheek throbbed with pain. He took his dick out? What is wrong with you Al you fucking prick!" She was livid!

"No I'm a man baby doll all man fully grown and more man then you ever had!" Camelo pressed his cheek against her left one, he hadn't shaved. I love you Mira..for realz. "Liar you love Charmaine! You just want to fuck me! "So." he laughed holding his dick. I got types baby and you one of them.".. "Fuck you!" Please do Mira he grabbed her sticking his tongue in her mouth! She slapped him! Let go you disgusting bastard! In a over whelming fit of anger she landed the hard ice pack to the back of his head, then smashing it into his face! He tossed it..laughing! "The girls was right about you! Mira said feeling sick to the stomach! Catching the straps to her blouse covering up her large breast. You just hire girls for sex!" He yanked Mira to him roughly this time hurting her arm. "Shut the fuck up Mira! You talk too much! He worked her pants down and stuck his hand in her drawls working them to her ankles! Camelo pressed her down to the floor. She felt sicker. But didn't have the strength to fight him off! "Stop it damn you!" she bit his large fingers before he started holding her mouth. Soon after that she felt penetration. Camelo licked her face straddling her fully clothed! He was horny. She cursed herself for already being wet from masturbating thinking about Wes. Camelo thought it was about him! I understand Wesley now why he had to have you! He humped kissing her all over her face. That nigga was so stoned and so drugged up at that party! He was unaware he had you and your sister up in that bed with him at the same time! Cause right after you passed out? Your little sister climbed on that bed on the other side of him and fucked him while you slept! That fucking Payton refuse to give it up for me! But she lost her virginity to the man who wanted to fuck her sister? You hoes are something else! Mira punched him over and over struggling against something she didn't want to remember! But he kept her pinned under his weight! Just then Lola happened to pass by the door. She heard noises coming from the other side, sex noises! She tip toed closer, slowly shoving the door. Lola blinked her eyes rapidly refusing to believe what she saw! Camelo was riding Mira on the floor! She threw the lamp at them! "You bitch!" she screamed at Mira as Camelo climaxed paying her no mind. You mutha fucker Camelo! You lied to me! Why ask me to come over if you already had somebody in here! And as for you Mira Charmaine was right to slap you! You two faced heffa! Mira tied her blouse back pulled up her pants up and got the hell out of there! Why waste her time trying to explain that she just been raped! Nobody would believe her! Camelo went up and kissed Lola like nothing happened. Girl she wasn't even that good, now you. He smiled kissing Lola. She giggled kissing him back.

"There was a lot of commotion going on outside in the hall. "It must be the dancers coming in for rehearsals, Lola tell him fixing herself."Shit!" Camelo groaned checking his watch. It was rehearsal time. All the other dancers ignored Mira burrowing a hole between them looking for a way out! Camelo went out looking for her until he spotted her. He caught up with her in the alley. And nosy Mona Ashford followed him of course. She knew every girl Al Camelo had slept with and was sure he now was hot after Mira! "Touche! " She tells Betty her best friend who ran up beside her. "I told you he was lying to Charmaine!" I guess you and me is too ugly for him!" Betty took that as an insult. "Meh he's not my type anyways too short. I'm taller then him! "Mona smirks at her. "Yeah right but Carl is your type and he's gay! You stupid he don't even know you alive" "And you do know he's sleeping with the piano player, don't you! "Why you gotta be a downer all the time Mona,that guy just don't know what he's missing...growl!" Mona rolled her eyes. "What?" Betty say shyly staring stooping next to her in the grass. "Will you please come all the way out lala land already! Girl Carl is not for you! Let's just get back you tall kangaroo!" Speak for yourself Mona the little hippo. "I am big boned and a better dancer than you!" Yeah right, you keep telling yourself that Mona! she laughed as they ran back into rehearsals.

"You'll move me and my mom out the slums." It was a statement. Camelo crept closer. "And right into Park View baby among the rich in Hopeful. If you keep quiet about this. Mira stared at him hard, she had lost all respect for Camelo. She turned away before clearing her throat! Mira please stay as one of my dancers! She couldn't believe she was seriously considering still working for the man who just raped her! "Just say yes." He pointed behind him at the club. I'm a business man first baby and you already know that about me! And I know when I see potential staring me in the face. You can grow here Mira! And when you dance with the girls you stand out! He whispered convincingly, handing her back the ice pack, she reclined. "Put it in writing." she tell him walking faster refusing to look back. Or even think about it another second! Because if she did then common sense would prevail and she couldn't have that! "Thank you..he smiled relieved wiping his forehead. Al walked backwards to the club checking her out. Those shapely legs was going in the opposite direction of him. Mira walked faster wishing her car hadn't been towed.

Chapter 15

The rain beat down on the slow moving vehicle behind her. "Looks painful" I said after rolling down my window. Come on get in you're getting drenched. "Mira stared saying nothing. She then put her hand on the handle getting in."I steered the wheel slowing this time noticing her giving me a peculiar look. She then made a unreadable expression. "What? I asked. Is something wrong?" Its nothing." she said. Old habits die hard she mumbled. I smiled over at her. "Its just that, I didn't think they had anymore gentlemen left in Hopeful. "Well then sorry to inform you,but I'm not from Hopeful. I'm from Colton its in Boston." She seemed to like my smile. I also think she thought she was talking to some naive hick who was green as grass. I really shouldn't disappoint the lady. " Yeah I keep hearing from the ladies around here that I'm a dinosaur." And man that hurt my feelings! I say placing my hand to my chest acting wounded. She hated me for making her laugh. "Just don't change." I found that a odd thing for her to say. "I won't." Mira held my eyes for more than a minute. And somehow I knew this was more than a chance between us. I wanted to see her again! "My house is in the next block, she pointed." I dropped her off in front her mama's house and she slid out. "Thank you and I don't think you're so dumb after all. The swelling in her face was gone but not the pain. She didn't offer a name. So I didn't pressed. Here I said. Giving her my card with the gold lettering. "If yo ever need a friend, call that number. "I will." she said taking it."Good night" she tells me walking up the steps in the drissle. "Good night I said disappointed with myself for not at least getting her name! I honked the horn waving. She turn back to me on the porch waving back. It felt good to meet a nice man, Mira was thinking. A man so very different from Camelo.

Inside she hurried over to her bathroom and for over an hour Mira sat in the tub soaking herself... crying. Charmaine had slapped her! Camelo had raped her! And in the midst of all that ugly she had met a nice man! The world was cruel! She wanted to bury herself under the floating bubbles and never come up!" Mira sat straight up in the tub soaking, getting angrier and angrier by the second. Her eyes burned. "Charmaine knew full well Camelo was having all those girls and was carrying on with Lola Bracken! Charmaine ranged her cell and Mira stared at it. It ranged eight times then stopped. Mira sat there watching the phone ring again. She then threw it upside the wall where it broke into pieces! Shit she would buy another! "Pick up hefa." Charmaine had said pacing, until she heard a weird buzzing noise coming from her phone. It then went dead. Something told her Mira must have busted the phone. "Well at least she's made it back home!" She tell Camay, who had just got back from her job at the boutique. "I mean Char you know we a small town. Shit they was even talking about y'all at my job!" Charmaine sat next to her sister on the sofa. "The thing is I wasn't really angry at Mira! I was mad at Camelo! And then I turned around and took it out on her! And I do regret doing that so much! "So she ain't speaking to you huh?" Nope. "Well give her a couple of days sis you two been friends since you both was five." Hey my birthday's coming up what you getting me!" Charmaine laughed at her happiness. "Nothing, she lied!" Camay pouted.."Whaaat?" Come on let's go to the Seafood Shack, my treat." O'kay! They left out running to Camay's sports car! Charmaine's house phone ranged, it was Mira. She hang up her land line phone slowly. Then stretched herself across her bed on her stomach falling asleep. One lingering tear fell onto her pillow.

Charmaine walked away from the stage, staring at all the dust on everything, she wiped her hands."Oh she knew Camelo couldn't commit to one woman to save his soul!" He lived by some man code! The one most men do. She just hated the fact that he couldn't stop staring at Mira. Or wanting her, a woman could tell! She knew she couldn't hurt him so she chose to hurt her best friend instead which was stupid! Mira and the girls was dancing on the stage rehearsing tonight, since the next day the police would close the club until they solved the murder. She took the towel offered her by one of the girls closer to the stage toweling off. Charmaine had come in staring around. Mira crossed her brows bawling up her fist, when Charmaine approached her. Charmaine ran into Mira's arms and hugged her really tight surprising her, in front of all those people. "I'm so sorry Mira, she gushed." Mira wanted to push her off. But she knew it took guts for Charmaine to do that. She squeezed her friend instead just as tight, letting the tears flow. Charmaine wiped them, smiling sincerely. "Do me a favor will you friend. If you ever see me acting that crazy again over a man? Please slap the shit out of me!" I sure will. Mira smiled, as they both laughed, listening to the other girls around them laughing in good spirits too. Charmaine was so happy they had made up. The next minute the unbelievable happened. The police came in heading straight for Mira turning her around! "You have the right to remain silent, they said cuffing her. And reading her, her rights! You have the right to a Attorney and so on. Mira said nothing while they handcuffed her. They took her away. Everybody in the place was mad! Some voiced their anger loudly! Others shook their fists at the Officers. Charmaine grabbed her by the shoulders. "I got you okay!"she said. Mira nodded at Charmaine. Charmaine then called her bank.

Chapter 16

"Hey." ...Yeah Chief I'm awake." Clara said groggily putting on her slippers. "Your hair is a mess, but you still a cutie my friend" Awww thanks Chief, she said smiling patting his cheek. He crumbled like a napkin does sipping more of my stale coffee. "For a broad light skinned guy the Chief turned into a pussy cat around the ladies. "Well at least your eyes are staring to look human again human being, he tells me." .. "Har har." I joked zipping up Clara's dress. "Why did you came back last night?" I asked in a low voice when the chief went back for coffee. She stared. "I really don't know." The tension between us was so tense and awkward and the silence so telling. "So where you headed today Clara?" The Chief asked. "Where else to Bowmen Street. "You don't have to come with me Miles, she quickly added. "Sleep in, you could use it." I gave her one of my sour puss expressions. "No I want to go." She put on her hat and fur. "Then don't hate me Miles for saying this. But I'm curious to hear what the woman who's managed to make a thousand dollar bail on a meager dancer salary has to say. After killing the owner of the Sienna Club..her Boss." From what I keep hearing, there's a pretty good chance she's guilty."

 I flipped the script while slipping into my blue suit. "You're talking about Mira?" I helped her into her green tweed coat. "Well yeah." I'm sorry you have to talk to her down at the station. "Yeah you know, she did make bail Clara, so why detain her? She and the Chief exchanged glances. "We got some questions we feel only she could answer Miles." The Chief answered instead. "I need to be there then." I walked off, they followed. You got to admit Miles, all the evidence is stacked against her!" "A garbage truck rolled by splattering the stinky puddle water that was turning into a pot hole, all over Clara's nice open toe shoes. "Fuck!" she cussed. The guy whistled at her without stopping. "Hey!" I yelled shaking a fist, coming to her defense. But that was all I could do. She frowned at me, then smiled planting a kiss. Clara just was so prim and proper so early in the morning and a beauty too. I wasn't worried for myself. I could get my old dogs washed for free down at Bill's Barber Shop. But women liked nice shoes. It was 5:o'clock and the sun was going down by the time we got to Bowman Street, The jail house loomed in front us. It felt like I'd been driving forever. The town maybe was small but the streets went on for miles! Did you get the pun miles? We did a pit stop first and went got some hamburgers and soda drinks, everybody was starving.

Camey run across the street totally worried she'd be late for work. Nature called and she had to do number two! Lana Lane was a thriving black owned boutique the only one in Hopeful. Mostly every black woman shopped there. It even had some white ladies, several Latina ladies and the occasional Asian ladies, not to mention the Indian and Muslim women who loved their dresses as well as their scarfs. A lot of ladies visited Lana Lane Boutique. Most only stopped by every once in a while tho. Like today because The Sweet Water Annual Ball was tomorrow. And the little shop was already buzzing and seeing an over flow of customers looking for ball gowns. "Gloria walked in the place looking all refreshed. She kept wishing her friend Clara would have went shopping with her but she understood her friend was a working woman. "Can I help you?" Camay asked pasting her customary smile. "You sure can Camay." Gloria smiled back. Payton came through the door just then, looking very smug and very rich. "Gloria" she said passing by her. "Payton" Gloria put up a hand in front her, she paused. "What is Gloria?" I'm so sorry to hear about your sister. "Payton stared at her folded hands. "Mira's a grown woman, she could handle this." You girls are so much like your mother. "Thank you." And can I say something without all the pleasantries Gloria." Sure. "I know you and Clara are friends. Gloria's expression changed, that's true. "I just want you know that Mira really cares about the detective. I think she's in love with him actually." Gloria saw Payton watching them closely. She was pasting price tags on dresses.

"I left Wes, we're getting a divorce." I'm really sorry to hear that." Don't be. He wasn't in love with me anyways. Mira took me and the kids in until I found a place. What I'm trying to say is she's very kind. So please don't judge her by what happened eight years ago. "I won't." Gloria promised, surprised to see Paton going towards the bargain section. Camay ran to the bathroom just then to wash her hands! Her boss Lana Lane followed her in. "Are you alright my dear?" She saw Camay vigorously washing her clean hands again and found it weird! "Yes ma'am!" Camay went back to acting normal like nothing happened. Lana stared at her . "You do know this is the fourth time I've seen you in here this week washing your clean hands like that." Camay smirked. "Its nothing Lana I must be getting a rash. "Do you guys have any new arrivals Camay?" Payton asked interrupting them when they came out the bathroom. Camay directed her to the more expensive ones. Camay and Payton was the same age. "Of course we do come on, she walked her to the back to get away from her boss. Then brought out some very beautiful long gowns and very expensive ones. Paytons eyes caught sight of a see through dark blue sheer gown with sliver matellics placed in very revealing places. "That one!" she brightened up opening her Prada bag giving Payton a money card. "Are you going to the Ball tomorrow?" She asked Camay. "I guess" Camay say without giving it much thought. Even us church girls like to dance you know. "Good." Payton tell her, taking her shopping bag. You should socialize more often. I'll introduce you to some people. "See you there." "Okay..she waved feeling like she just made a new friend.

When we walked in we saw Mira seated at the interrogation table. She made no motion towards me this time. Clara gave me a bewildered look. "I would never know it was because Mira saw Clara's car parked in front my apartment after 2 am last night. Her attitude was cool also. I sat across from her, she hung her head refusing to look at me. The Chief sat next to Clara. Then Clara decided to stand. "Whats this about?" Mira put the question to the Chief, she was angry. "The surveillance tape Ms. Sylvester." She smiled up at us. I have nothing to say. May I leave now?" The Chief motioned to the officer by the door. "Bring in Rufus." Mira's mouth fell open, she even stood when he came in. "Hey Mira." he said surprised to see her. They nod at each other. I didn't like it. "Rufus, we got the two of you on tape." He blew the Chief off paying him no mind. What I should have said is, the Chief stood remembering who he was and his authority. We got you, Mira, Mira's mother and your sister Camay on tape." Mira closed her eyes as Rufus cocked his head up at the Chief. "Man you guys are way off!" he was literally shaken you could see it. And the nervous laugh didn't help. That's all." the Chief tell him. "Take him back." he tell the officer. Rufus reached for Mira's hand holding it., before leaving out. The Chief turned to Mira, you're free to go Ms. Sylvester. Mira's legs felt like lead. "Thanks for the heads up." Clara tells her just before she close the door. I took this opportunity to get some answers of my own. "Okay Clara, what's up with all this hostility I'm seeing from you towards Mira. "None of your business. Arent you going to go behind your girl? Clara ignored me and started fixing the papers on the table. "Mira slept Wesley Sweetwater Miles." the Chief said regardless of the fact Clara looked betrayed! "What?" I tell him. Wesley was drugged and ended up in the bed with Mira and her sister Payton eight years ago at the Sweetwaters Anual Ball. Clara walked out. I took a seat I had too. The Chief left me there grabbing his coat and hat. "I'll be in the car Miles."

The Sweetwater's Annual Ball was that night..
And I had never seen anything so beautiful in my entire life! I had a feeling all the culprits would be there. And they was. I spotted Clara walking around. She had on a stunning gown! It was all white and it glimmered. It suited her. Wesley came up to me, following my eyes over to Clara. "Beautiful isn't she?" he offered a drink, I declined. Marco wasn't far I observed his disappointing face when I turned the drink down. "She's mine detective Wes say next as if giving me an ultimatum. "You sure about that?" I said walking away letting him chew on those apples. Mira had arrived and if there was such a thing as a angel. she would be first in line to receive her wings. "Jesus that light green form fitting ball gown with the back fully exposed woke my manhood. And I was sure I wasn't the only one. The Chief came through the door with his gorgeous wife Gloria. They was the epitome of a married couple. The Chief shined in his gray tux. I think I did alright my dark blue tux had that satin sash around the midsection. And the ladies kept staring at me. I fixed me a drink when the music started. Of course all the couples made it to the center of the floor. Marco kept running upstairs. This time he came back down with Vincent they was in a deep conversation. "Dance with me." Mira asked taking my hand. "I felt the silkiness of her skin and smelled the perfume scent and wanted to forget about the case! We waltzed she was elated to see I didn't miss a beat! "You are something Miles she smiled."

Her hair was down and it was styled with very little curls around the front she was the word beautiful. Clara walked up to us. "May I?" she say to Mira cutting in taking my hand. Everybody stared even

Vincent Sweetwater. "Mira reluctantly backed away. "Clara stared right into my eyes when we started to waltz. "I love you." she said to me right in front of Mira. Gloria smiled. Clara left the floor. Camay came with Payton and some of Payton's friends. Stay right here." she tell Camay running over to the pnch bowl. She was talking to a yong man standing there filling his red cp. "She returned with him they was in good spirits. "We can talk later Olsen." she tells him batting mischievous. "This is my friend Camay. "Camay this is Olsen Sweetwater he's twenty. "The youngest Sweetwater and the nicest. "That's right bild me p! he laughed taking her gloved hand. Camay had on a long pink chiffon gown something a girl wold wear to a prom certainty not a ball! Bt it didn't seem to bother Olsen in the least. The both of them went over to a corner pleasantly getting to know one another. He gave her his drink, she smiled. Payton was all for this match! Yet she still went looking for her husband Wes. I couldn't stop thinking about Clara although Mira was right next to me. One lady called us a couple as we passed them. Payton came through the door earlier in that see through gown which left very little to the imagination! She was looking around for Wes from the moment she got there. She wanted to get a rise out of him with her sexy outfit! The girl had a warm smile for everyone she talked too yet inside she longed to get back with husband. When she did see Wes, he was coming towards her with Keke on his arms! Payton's smile was gone for the rest of the night. I was sure Mira was sticking to me like glue because of Clara. When I saw Clara next she was standing way to back behind a crowd. I think she was staring at Mira and I but wasn't sure. Somebody pressed a song on the jute box. It was Barry White singing My First, My Last, My Everything. All the couples hit the floor laughing and dancing! Mira took my hands and led me out to the floor. I smiled keeping up with the tempo. I wasn't aware that Clara had started slowly walking towards us. Gloria smiled crossing both her fingers placing it against her chest as if praying. Mustard stared down at his wife. Something was happening but what? Clara was slowed down by the the people having fun dancing in the isles! But she struggled on. The piano player Dalton stood smiling. "You go girl! he whispered. Carl even smiled, he was cleaning a glass. Mira saw Clara before I did. She had stop laughing and dancing her smiled even dropped. "I love you." Clara say to me, before running towards the exit! Mira stood there motionless, then stared over at me. For once I had my eyes on Clara. I smiled.

 Vincent made his way to the middle of the floor and Mira whispered in my ear that she'd be back. Vincent Sweetwater clicked a fork to his glass calling for everyone's attention. "We have a special treat for you guys tonight! His voice boomed in the microphone. We have the dancers of the infamous Sienna Club to entertain you tonight! It was the first time I saw Mira and the dancers perform. Hopeful showed the girls some love. And even their very own.. Mira! He pointed to the tiny stage as everyone gathered around it. I made my way through the crowd. Mira was dancing like I had never seen her before. She nailed that dance! Mira got screams from the enthused crowd! But kept her eyes on me, I bowed and she smiled happily. I then noticed Dalton had joined the conversation with Marcos and Carl. All of a sudden Dalton jet out of there with his forehead veins popping out he was so angry! He spotted me in the crowd and reached me something out his pocket! "You need to see this detective! I'm the informant your Chief told you about! "Thank you Dalton" I said. He left with an even angrier Carl chasing behind him! Marco was furious, he got his coat and left! The party was indeed beautiful but there was a lot of ugly going on. Mira joined me after she changed back into her gown. A lot of people was coming up telling her how great she was. Finally she was receiving the respect from her hometown, she deserved. I gotta go I tell her running out of there with the envelope in my hand. The next morning everything would come to a head! I got a call from the undercover cop. She told me the Chief had Mira and Rufus in the interrogation room again. He and Clara had found what they was looking for! In the mean time I had a piece of the tape not even the Chief was aware of. I took a seat right across from Mira. Still standing by her. Mira was wringing her hands out nervously staring over at Clara. Rufus had eyes only for Mira. Mira's mother was brought in. Salita sat next to her daughter. Mira didn't like this one bit! Camay was then brought in. And Rufus hopped up cursing! "Naw dog you tripping!" He said with the hand cuffs on top his head about to lose it! By the time Camay took a seat, she was already shaking and beginning to cry. Everyone was seated by now.

Epilogue

The Chief motioned for another officer to turn on the video. "Rufus and Mira watched it to my surprise, very intensely. "Camay had come in while Camelo was eating supper. He was cutting his stake and followed it with a glass of red wine. They turned up the part where she was heard talking. "I said stop fucking over my sister!" You ain't nothing but low life trash Camelo! And Char deserves better! Listen to me when I'm talking to you scum!" Camelo wiped his lips on a napkin., laughing. "Why you wasting my time little girl ha Camay? Can't you see I'm a busy man! He shouted that last part, making her jump nervously a little bit! "Camay go home..he tells her still chewing his food. Go watch some cartoons or something he laughed. "I'm a grown woman you idiot!" she shouted. "Oh yeah!" he rushed towards her pulling her into him! "What do you want from me little girl, do you want me to fuck you!" She slapped him. He kissed her and she responded. Circling her arms around his waist! Camay wanted to lose her virginity! She wanted to be a woman like Charmaine and Mira! She wanted to be desired by men! "Camelo pushed her off. "I could still smell the breast milk. Look just go home already! Git the fuck outta here!

 "You can screw my sister or Mira or any one of these slutty hoes in here but you going to refuse me! "He yanked her by the arm. "Git your ass home now little girl cause your folks raised you!" I'm grown! she barked showing him her breast! "Camelo laughed at them. "Get the fuck out Camay while I'm being nice! Come back when that pussy between your legs is as long as my hand okay! He said putting up a hand laughing! Now fuck out of here and stop embarrassing Charmaine!" She screamed grabbing the knife off his plate. Camelo turned around she buried the knife in his chest! Camelo's blood shoot out and splattered all over her hands! "Oh my god! Oh my god!"she trembled shaking uncontrollably! "Mira's mother Salita had also decided to have a talk with Camelo she didn't want her daughter working for him! Salita had opened the door finding Camay on her knees crying over Camelo. She walked towards her in a state of shock! "What happened?" she whispered staring down at him. "I..I..don't know!" Camay dropped the bloody knife out her hands. Salita's head came up as Rufus came through the door. He had followed her afraid she was going to do something stupid. "Sis what the hell!" She was sitting there shaking with the front of her dress covered in blood! "Rufus bent down wiping her hands on his shirt. "Rufus I think she stabbed him" Salita tells him. Rufus stared around, he needed to think! "Sis why!" she was sobbing saying nothing. "My god!" They here from over by the door. Mira was walking towards them shaking like a leaf!

"What happened?" she stared at Camelo, he wasn't moving. "Rufus stood Camay up. "Miss. Salita get her out of here please!" He opened the window. "Rufus I..I didn't mean too!" He hugged his baby sister. "I know Camay but right now you got to go okay!" Rufus helped Camay and Salita climb out the window. They ran across the street! "He was on stooping on the floor staring up at Mira. "Mira find the knife!" They looked for it but couldn't find it anywhere. People started coming towards the back! And they heard a police unit pulled up soon after! "Get out of here Mira! "Rufus shouted. Hurry up get out now! Mira was wool gathered. "But what about you, you got blood all over you Rufus!" Listen never mind me, he kissed her on the lips. Please get out of here baby I hear the cops and I'll have kill somebody if they hurt you! "Then be careful" she said holding onto his hand. You too he said. "Clara eyes was resting on Miles. She could tell he wasn't taking this very well!" Rufus climbed up in the window, after watching Mira run out. That was the only time Mira's eyes met mine. The Chief clicked off the tape. That was my cue to leave. "Miles!" I hear her call after me. Rufus ignored us he was pointing in the chief face! "If this don't go down as self defense I'll kill all you muthefuckas! Camay's head was in her hands. One of the officers stood her up cuffing her. "No!" Rufus yell. "Its okay brother..she sobbed I'm a woman now." Clara felt so sorry for all three of them, yes and even Mira. "You will be released as soon as we're done with the paper work Rufus." The Chief left. " Mira hugged Rufus, he breathed a sign of relief before they took him away. Salita followed behind them glancing back only once at her daughter. "I'm going to cook a big dinner tonight. "I'll be there mama. Mira hugged her. Salita sniffed. "Good."

Clara said hey you, to Mira. I never thought I would have respect for you. But I do today. You and Rufus was ready to go down for Camay. You guys was willing to sacrifice everything even your lives for her! "She's very young."Mira say with her mind on me. "I respect you too Detective Clara, she finally said. They shared a smiled. "Take care of him, Mira tell her." I will, Clara say without any remorse. Mira ran to catch up to Rufus. She walked beside him with the officers. Clara was surprised to see Charmaine joined them. She had followed Camay and had been standing in the door the whole time looking at the tape. She caught up to Rufus and walked on the other side of her brother. She never felt so much pride for him, as she do now. And somehow she knew after his release. They will all stand in solidarity with their sister Camay. And Mira will be right there with them. Rufus shed tears. He was not alone, he was not alone, he was with family. "He maybe had lost out on one of his biggest dreams. But he still had these two strong women beside him. Charmaine gave Mira a high five, she smiled.

Outside Clara spotted me leaning against the wall watching them take Camay to prison and Rufus to be set free. I saw the closeness between Rufus and Mira at last on that tape. Clara stood in front of me. "Hey its over." Not exactly I tell her. I was given the missing piece to the tape. Mira stared over at me before getting in her car, I waved. She smiled and waved back. "What do you mean not exactly?" Clara was forever the gumshoe. She wasn't aware of Mira and me. The Chief is watching it now, I said throwing down my cigarette bud. "Camay gave Camelo a flesh wound. But Marco killed him. Clara leaned into the wall beside me. "What!"she was shocked! At the ball last night Dalton handed me the missing piece to the tape. Marco was having a secret relationship with Dalton. Carl found out and all hell broke loose! Carl's mistake was trusting Marcos. Marcos told Dalton he killed Camelo! Carl couldn't stand Camelo. "I know that Miles, but why would Marco kill his half brother?" Because Camelo became the millionaire he wanted to be, its as simple as that. He wanted the Sienna Club back. But knew Camelo wouldn't give it to him. So he saw his opportunity when Camay stabbed his brother. The reason nobody could find the knife was because Marco had it. Clara couldn't believe how this case was unfolding. She removed her hat staring at it. "Marco knew he was home free because Camay had Camelo's blood on her hands. He on the other hand wore gloves. He used the fact that the police was busy outside arresting Rufus and questioning Mira. Marco slipped out the back door unnoticed. He had found the knife and stabbed Camelo in the stomach with it eight more times. You know how we got him? Clara stared, how? He was crying while killing his brother. He actually cared about Camelo, but the money meant more. There was tear stains on the front of Camelo's clothes. Perfect DNA. "Unbelievable." fell from Clara's lips. And all for money. And all for money, I repeated her words. Clara then noticed I was holding a box. "What's that?".. "Here." she stared at me smiling before opening it. It was shoes! The same kind she had on. The ones the garbage truck splashed all that mud on and ruined this morning. I bend taking off the muddy shoes, putting on the new ones. Clara stared down at me. "Oh you are getting so laid. "I love you too." I said taking her in my arms. She then gave me one of those long lingering satisfying kisses I was use too. We walked in the direction of my car. "I don't know Miles they feel kinda small."..she complained. "I could take them back." .."Don't you dare!" she walked limping! The Chief had came out he was laughing at us, putting his hat on his head before pulling out in his squad car.

The End